A BROOKHAVEN PARANORMAL COZY MYSTERY
BOOK 5

HIGH HARVEST

S.E. BIGLOW

SPECIAL THANKS

I would like to thank all of the wonderful backers who supported this series on Kickstarter and made these books possible.

I need to give an extra special shout out to Jean Sitkei, Monica Kim, Anonymous Reader, Anonymous, Kathryn, Sara Vath, jeffrey.tristan.thyme, Ryan Scott James, GhostCat, Louisa, Rebecca Carter, Tory Penfield, Margaret M. St. John, Chloe Campbell, Heiko Koenig, Tom S., Alexandra Corrsin, Francesco Tehrani, maileguy, Rosie Pease, Sketch, Ernie Ridley, Amelia Pluck, Ayl, John Idlor, Sandy K., Brian D. Lambert, Michelle Kaye, Bonniejean Boettcher, Nicole Valdez, Eva S., Megan, Voldane Pelt, Diane Wagoner, Katrina, Rebecca Bock, Karin Baxter, Krista abd Barbara Griffiths, Jennifer Herschbach, Lisa Spalding, Sam, Isaac Dansicker, PippiMD, Brian, Rayne Sinclair, Mike Jones, Katie, Cheryl, Leslie, Nicole, Melissa, Vi Ta, Beth Caudill, Jennifer

Preslar, Sasha Washburn, Matthew Walker, Jackie Ewing, Jenna N., Stephen Ballentine, Melissa Showers and Rob Steinberger

1

The seasons had shifted again, catapulting the small town of Brookhaven squarely into summer heat. Trees were lush with leaves and flowers bloomed everywhere I looked. For a hedge witch, this was practically paradise. To think only a year ago, this would have driven me mad. Oh, how far I'd come in such a short time. I'd made this place my home and created a comfortable existence for myself among its inhabitants.

"You look like you're in a good mood, Darcy," my co-worker Thomas noted as I stood in front of my locker in the break room of High Time, the town's marijuana dispensary.

I had just finished the end of my shift tending

the dispensary's marijuana crop and I had plans. "Maggie and I are going away overnight. Well for the weekend, really," I answered.

Thomas leaned against the open door of his locker, his dark dreads hanging in his eyes. "Your first vacation together? That's a pretty big step. You learn a lot about people when you're crammed into a hotel room."

"It's just an excursion to Haven Island. One of the rich blokes is renting their house out to vacationers and we decided we'd give it a try." Besides, it wasn't like we were moving in together.

Not that the topic hadn't come up. A few months back, Maggie had made an offer that I could at the very least leave some clothes at her apartment, given that I was spending more time there. I hadn't been ready for that level of commitment. And I still wasn't quite there, yet.

"Darcy, you're still here? I thought you guys were heading out?" Sage, the dispensary owner, said, appearing from the back office. Her vibrant aqua hairdo had transitioned to a more lime green to match the new glasses she'd gotten.

"It's like you lot don't want me here," I said with a laugh. "I'm going, I'm going."

In truth, I still needed to stop back at Tania's

B&B to get my bag before meeting Maggie at the hospital. She served as the town's magical healer, but over the last few months, she'd taken an interest in more traditional medicine. One of the Emergency Room doctors had agreed to let her shadow some of his shifts.

I closed the door to my locker and bid my colleagues goodbye before heading out through the kitchen where the bakers were winding down for the day. I left the dispensary behind, making the short trek back to the B&B on Main Street. To my surprise, summertime wasn't a big draw for the area. At least not for tourists looking to stay for more than day trips. Somehow, Tania got by in the interim and I couldn't deny that I enjoyed the bit of peace and quiet in the house. I entered the front hall to find my landlord and friend, Tania standing at the foot of the stairs leading up to the second and third floors. She was talking to what appeared to be an empty spot on the railing.

"No, I haven't noticed anything," she told the seemingly empty air.

I watched as the wood's smooth grain shifted, taking on the ripple of scales as Beau dropped his invisibility. Even after nearly a year in town, I still didn't know how the chameleon had come to reside at Tania's B&B. She'd never shared the details either, only assuring me he was a friend that he'd taken a shine to me.

His magic, and his guidance, had come in handy on a number of occasions when I'd found myself deep in the heart of a mystery.

"Am I interrupting?" I called, drawing their attention.

"No. Beau is just being overly cautious," Tania answered.

Mundane people might ask how she could read a chameleon's emotional state. Tania was an empath and her abilities extended to most living creatures in the same way that my plant magic connected me to the tiniest blade of grass all the way to the largest tree.

"He hasn't mentioned anything to me," I said, stepping up to stand beside Tania. "You holding out on me, mate?"

'Something is hunting.'

Even I could feel the anxiety in his telepathic words. "Can you be more specific?"

Beau's head waved side to side in a 'no' gesture. I turned to Tania. "And you haven't noticed anything strange?"

"No. Everything has felt normal for once."

"Try not to worry, Beau. I'm sure everything's fine," I said, giving him a gentle pat on the head. "I've got to get my bag and then meet Maggie."

Tania's lips quirked into a smile. "You're excited. I'm so happy things are working out well with you two."

"So am I," I admitted. Sometimes I still felt nervous around Maggie, it being my first serious relationship in years.

'*Well suited together,*' Beau chimed in.

"Thanks for the vote of confidence, mate. It really means a lot," I said, giving the chameleon another stroke on the back. "But honestly, you don't need to worry. We're just going to Haven Island for a couple of days."

"Oh, how quickly she forgets," chirped Sam, materializing a few steps above Tania.

I glanced up at the B&B's resident ghost, taking in his sequined jacket with velvet collar in a bright lime green. His eyeliner was thicker than usual. "I haven't forgotten anything," I retorted.

How could I have forgotten that not quite a year ago, my first trip to the small island off the coast of Brookhaven had sent me crashing into another murder mystery. But things had been quiet for months and there'd been no reports of anything suspicious on the island since Captain Merchant's ill-fated attempt to get out of paying alimony.

"Both of you, behave," Tania chided in a motherly tone, eyeing first Sam and then me. She gestured to me and then up the stairs. "Go on, get your things. You shouldn't keep Maggie waiting."

I bounded up the stairs and grabbed my already-packed overnight bag. I double checked that the tickets for the stay were secure in the front zipper compartment before I slung it over my shoulder and returned to the first floor. Sam had moved down to hover by the front desk where Tania kept the logbook of guests.

"Try to stay out of trouble while I'm gone," I told him with a wink.

"And here I was going to tell you not to do anything I wouldn't do," he replied with a cheeky grin.

I left the B&B behind, shaking my head at his comment. For someone who could literally be in anyone's business without many of them being the wiser, Sam was incredibly private about both his life and the circumstances surrounding his death. Plus, he was the only ghost I'd met since moving here. One day, I'd get him to spill all of the details. But not today.

I shifted my overnight bag to the other shoulder as I crossed Main Street and made my way toward the hospital. I'd been surprised to find the town had one. When I'd first moved to town, I'd assumed that Maggie's clinic was the primary source of medical care for the residents. But my adventures with my cousin Piper four months ago had proved that Brookhaven did in fact boast a fully functioning hospital, complete with a robust Emergency Department.

Though I felt a little awkward walking in and approaching the nurse's station. This was where I expected to find my girlfriend. Thankfully, it was relatively empty. The charge nurse looked up at me through thick-rimmed glasses.

"You need to check in at the front," she said, gesturing back the way Id' come.

"Sorry, I'm looking for Maggie Lawson. She's been shadowing one of the doctors on rounds today," I explained.

"Which doctor?"

"I've got it from here, Grace," a semi-familiar male voice called from behind me.

I turned to find the doctor who'd taken care of Piper back in March. He was handsome, if a little pale, with vibrant green eyes and thick dark hair. He closed the distance and held out his hand. "Dr. Elijah Fitz."

"Right. Sorry," I said, shaking his hand.

"Maggie's just changing out of her scrubs. She'll be ready in a minute," he said, shoving his hands in his pockets.

"Thanks. I'll just go wait in the lobby," I said.

He reached out, faster than I would have thought possible, and grabbed my arm to keep me where I stood. "No need. Here she comes."

I turned to look over my right shoulder to see Maggie leaving a back area, bag on her own shoulder. She'd exchanged the pale blue medical scrubs for a loose-fitting top and a pair of denim shorts. A pair of sunglasses sat perched atop her short-cropped auburn hair.

"You sure you don't mind me ducking out early?" Maggie addressed Dr. Fitz.

"I'm about to go off the clock. You're fine. Besides, you deserve a chance to have some fun."

"What about the patient in four?" Maggie gestured to one of the curtained treatment bays.

"Just a few stitches. I'll wrap it up. You two go. Enjoy your weekend," Dr. Fitz insisted.

Her dedication to her patients was one of the many things I loved about Maggie. I would have expected nothing less than concern about leaving a patient not fully attended.

"If, you're sure." She still didn't look convinced as I slid my hand into hers and tugged her toward the exit.

"We're going to miss our boat," I prompted her.

She gave me a sideways look and an arched brow. "Words I never thought you'd be saying."

I was not the world's biggest fan of water. In the last year, Maggie had insisted that I was suffering from a mild case of hydrophobia. Having come to blows with an elemental water witch last fall hadn't helped matters. But I wanted to spend the weekend alone with her in a fancy mansion and if that meant enduring a half hour on the relatively calm waters between Brookhaven and Haven Island, I'd manage.

"Think of it as conquering my fear," I said.

"I'm proud of you." She gave my hand a squeeze as we made our way to the boardwalk and the waiting charter.

For a brief moment, I couldn't help but flash back to the last time I'd gone on an excursion to the island. Nearly a year ago, I'd been on a day cruise that ended with one of the passengers turning up dead on the beach.

Get a grip, Darcy. That's not going to happen twice.

Yet, I couldn't' shake Beau's concern that something dangerous was lurking. Maybe I should have let him come along after all. I swallowed the lump in my throat as we boarded the charter boat and found seats below deck. I picked a spot near the window so I could see out. The water buoyed the hull with soft lapping sounds as we waited to pull anchor.

"I'm really glad we're doing this," Maggie murmured, resting her head on my shoulder. She still hadn't released her grip on my hand.

I appreciated the support and turned to kiss her forehead. "Me, too."

There were only a few other folks on the boat and as my phone showed the time ticking past two o'clock, the boat pulled away from the dock. Breath hitched in my throat momentarily as we hit a bit of rough water. The ride smoothed out after another few minutes and I felt myself beginning to relax. I shifted in my seat as the island came into view in the distance. From the last time I'd set foot there, I'd learned that it was under the jurisdiction of Brookhaven's police force and that most of the residents were extremely rich and reclusive. The fact that someone was opening up their home for overnight guests felt like a big deal.

"Is this the first time they're doing this getaway?" I asked, focusing on Maggie.

"Yeah, as far as I know. From what I've heard around town the owners aren't as well off as they like people to think and they need the extra income."

By around town, I had no doubt she meant someone had told Ginny Hayes that information and she'd heard it from her. Ginny was a witch like me and Maggie, but she trafficked information, specifically the truth. Just by being in her presence, people tended to admit things they might otherwise keep to themselves. Part of me wondered why anyone would frequent her café knowing that. But then, not everyone in town believed that magic was real.

"Well, even if that's true, we get a nice weekend out of it," I said. The shoreline grew larger as we closed the distance. I was ready for a drama-free weekend. I closed my eyes and put that desire out into the ether. I wasn't above trying to manifest what I wanted.

The boat eased to a stop at the edge of the beach and the other patrons disembarked, leaving Maggie and I alone below deck. I stood first and shouldered my bag walking up the steps to the upper deck and the gangplank leading to the beach. Maggie trailed me a moment later and as our feet touched the sand, I spotted a face I wouldn't have expected to see, Corinne.

The dead body on the beach a year ago had been her ex-husband's attempt to scupper his need to pay alimony payments. I was glad to see her still employed. I noted she'd traded in her stilettos for more sensible flats this time around. She noticed me in the small knot of people and gave me a small nod of acknowledgement.

"All right everyone, welcome to Haven Island. Please follow me, I'll take you up to your lodgings for the weekend."

She led us past Ollie's Oddities and The Tea Shoppe—both of which I was pleased to see were still open for business—and onto one of the designated walking paths to a cordoned off area. We stopped at the foot of a paved driveway, and I could make out a four-story house set back against a protective copse of trees.

"For the duration of the weekend, you will be hosted at Fairchild Manor. You're welcome to come and go as you please, but meals will be provided on the premises. I do need to remind you that all of the other private residences are off-limits to the public,"

Corrine announced before she undid the cordon and led us up the drive.

As I glanced around the area, I couldn't help but feel a blanket of unease settle over me. I closed my eyes and tried to reach the greenery around me, urging them with my magic to give me a hint if something bad was on the horizon.

Nothing appeared to be out of place.

"You look worried," Maggie whispered in my ear as she nudged my shoulder to keep me moving.

"Sorry. Being back here is more unnerving than I expected. Just trying to reacquaint myself with the local flora."

"This trip is meant to be relaxing. No magic allowed. For either of us," Maggie said as she tugged me along up the driveway and through the manor's front doors.

2

I could have fit most of the first floor of Tania's B&B in the entry hall of the Fairchild Manor. The flooring was polished grey and white marbled granite with two large, curved staircases ascending along the outer walls up to the second floor.

"I'm dreaming," I whispered as Maggie took my hand and urged me deeper into the house.

"You're not" she assured me.

Footsteps came ahead of us and Corinne appeared, waving us on. "I'm just starting the tour," she called. Her voice echoed in the cavernous entry hall as Maggie and I followed her through the arch of the staircases.

She led us into a kitchen with three ovens and

more gleaming counter space than I thought possible. In my mind's eye, I pictured staff hustling and bustling in the space to prepare elaborate meals for the family that lived here. The vision popped like a bubble when I realized that the family who owned the manor was in financial straits.

"You have access to whatever you'd like. Unfortunately, we were only able to secure staff for dinner. So, you're on your own making breakfast. We do have a small catered lunch each day, as well," Corrine explained to the other couples who'd come over with us on the boat.

There was an older couple, both with greying temples who stood off to one side, taking in not the expansive space but the rest of us. I locked gazes with the woman and barely repressed a shiver. She looked at me like I didn't belong here. After a moment, I broke eye contact, taking a half-step closer to Maggie until I felt the gentle pressure of her forearm brush against mine.

Then there was the newlywed couple who couldn't seem to keep their hands off each other. The guy pulled his wife close and made a sweeping gesture toward one of the ovens.

"I'll cook you breakfast every morning, babe," he professed.

"Ronnie, that's so sweet," she gushed, and pulled him in for another prolonged kiss.

Corinne cleared her throat and pivoted. "If you'd come with me upstairs, I'll show you to your rooms."

I hurried to catch up with our hostess, Maggie hot on my heels. She slipped her hand into mine, so we didn't get separated as we walked back through the entry hall and climbed the right hand staircase to the second floor.

"How long have you been hosting these events?" I asked, falling into step beside Corrine.

"Oh, the last six months I guess."

"You probably don't remember me," I continued. "I actually met you last year during a day excursion."

Corinne turned and her gaze narrowed as she studied me. "You do look a little familiar."

"I sort of helped the police catch your ex-husband after he killed one of his passengers," I explained.

Her eyes widened as recognition dawned. "Yes, I do remember you now." She smoothed the front of her dress. "Uh ... That was not a great time for me."

"I didn't mean to make things uncomfortable. I just meant that I'm glad you're doing so well after everything."

She gave me a weak smile. "Thank you. Come on, let's get you to your rooms."

To my surprise there was yet another curving staircase that led us up to the third floor with a wing of spacious bedrooms. When Corinne stopped and gestured to the one closest to the stairs, my jaw went slack.

"Enjoy your stay."

She hurried off to settle the other couples, leaving Maggie and I standing in the doorway, taking in the king-size bed and delicate curtains. Maggie bumped my shoulder. "What are you thinking?"

"That I don't ever want to leave this room again."

Her laughter filled my ears, and I joined in as we crossed the threshold and shut the door. This trip was going to be exactly what we needed.

DESPITE THE COMFORTABLE BED AND THE SPACIOUS accommodations, I slept poorly that night. Beau's voice echoed through my dreams, warning of danger. Oh, why had I insisted on getting in the middle of his and Tania's discussion yesterday? I would have been better off just getting my things and leaving to pick up Maggie. I let out a groan and rolled over to find Maggie sound asleep, snoring softly into her pillow. I brushed a short lock of red hair off her forehead and quietly went in search of clean clothes.

Once dressed, I headed down to the kitchen in the hopes of finding an already-brewed pot of coffee. My phone told me it was only seven o'clock, so I doubted the newlyweds would be up and about yet. But the older couple might be early birds. Not that I fancied breakfast under that woman's judgmental gaze.

I found the kitchen empty. I was apparently the first person awake in the manor. So, I set about making myself some eggs and coffee. I found some fresh berries in one of the industrial fridges and settled in for my meal.

No one else joined me. Once I'd finished my eggs and coffee, I set to doing the dishes. I considered retreating to the room to see if Maggie was awake yet. But she deserved to sleep in. She'd been pushing herself with all the hours she'd put in at the hospital. Besides, I'd hardly had the chance to explore the island properly on my last excursion.

I left the manor behind, strolling at a leisurely pace down the drive to the gate which kept nosy visitors at bay. The morning air was salty and crisp. Even this far inland from the beach, I could still taste it on my lips as I inhaled. I eased the gate open and made sure it shut behind me before I wandered in the direction of the beach. I passed The Tea Shoppe, still closed for the morning, and paused at Ollie's Oddities, not expecting it to be open this early. Yet, the eponymous Ollie sat behind the counter nursing a thermos of what I assumed to be coffee.

"Don't I know you?" he called before I had a chance to pass by his shop.

"Uh ... well, we've met before. I was on the island last year when that woman got killed," I said, stepping into the doorway. For once he didn't have the air conditioning blasting.

"Oh, yeah. That's right. What brought you back?"

"One of the families that owns property on the island is renting out their home for the weekend. My girlfriend and I took a weekend trip away."

He looked sullen at the fact rich people were renting their homes. "It's been a good run, but I suspect we'll be seeing more of that."

"What makes you say that?" I probed.

"Oh, just the people who own homes out here aren't exactly spring chickens, if you catch my drift.

And their relatives aren't going to want to do the upkeep on the properties."

"And you think that will decrease the tourists' desire to come visit," I concluded, and he nodded.

"Part of the allure of this place is it boasts private rich folks. When they leave, the attraction vanishes and the tourists realize we're just a little island with crappy Wi-Fi," he admitted.

"Well, I'm happy to do my part to keep things afloat," I said.

I stopped short of adding that the lack of murders had to be a positive as well. I was about to resume my trek down to the beach when something caught my attention. No, that wasn't quite right. It was like a tiny voice calling out in pain. The fact Ollie hadn't reacted suggested it was my special connection to the local flora that had triggered the voice.

"I should let you enjoy your coffee in peace," I said hurriedly and stepped out of the doorway.

I made it a few paces beyond Ollie's view before I allowed myself to focus on the cries of a plant somewhere on the island. I closed my eyes, trying to reach out and find it. I'd been able to track the origin of plants before, but that was only when I had a piece of what I was looking for. Instead of homing in on the specific plant, all I got was that steady pain. Eventually, that died down, too.

I found myself rubbing at my temple, as if I was the one who'd been in pain. The experience left me dazed and a little mentally foggy. Taking a solo trip to the beach suddenly felt like a poor decision. Besides, maybe Maggie would have an idea of what had happened or at least give me something to ease this headache. I made my way back toward the manor and nearly collided with Ronnie as he fumbled with the latch on the gate at the bottom of the drive.

"Morning," I greeted, trying to be cheerful and hide the fact my head throbbed like someone was using it as a drum.

Ronnie spun; eyes wide in surprise when he saw me. His confusion slowly gave way to vague recognition. "Oh, uh, morning." He tried to shield his left arm from view.

"Is everything all right?" I asked, undoing the latch so he could go up the driveway.

"Totally. Just out for an early morning walk."

"Without your wife?" I prodded.

"Mindy? She's not a morning person," he said, inching up the drive, but still concealing whatever he carried in his left hand.

"It's really sweet you offered to make her breakfast," I said. As I fell into step beside him, a wave of phantom pain washed over me. Somehow, I masked my distress.

He wasn't fast enough to keep what he carried out of sight this time. I spotted a handful of freshly cut roses with thorns still intact. He sported a few cuts on his hand too.

"You're not going to be able to cook with your hand like that."

"I'm fine," he replied.

"Come on, let's see if we can find some first aid to get you patched up. You don't want Mindy worrying," I urged. "And we can get those in some water."

"You promise you won't tell anyone where I got them?"

I pressed my lips into a thin line and simply nodded as he handed them over. I was careful to avoid the prickly spots on the stems, hurrying inside to find something to serve as a temporary vase. I plucked a single leaf from one of the flowers when Ronnie wasn't looking and slid it into my pocket.

I steered him into the kitchen, hoping it would yield a first aid kit. We found Maggie standing in front of the stove making pancakes. The eggs I'd whipped up earlier felt like I'd had them days ago.

"What's going on here?" Maggie asked, eyeing the fact I was holding Ronnie's wrist.

"Bit of an accident. We're in search of some bandages."

"I'll get you taken care of," Maggie said, slipping into healer mode.

With Ronnie safely in Maggie's care, I slipped back out of the manor and cupped the leaf in my palm. "Let's see where you came from."

The pain I'd sensed earlier finally receded enough for my head not to feel like it was about to burst when my magic connected with the leaf. I opened my eyes, and my gaze was tinted green as if I were seeing through the leaf's perspective. It was an experience I'd only done once before, and it was unnerving. Still, I allowed the magic to guide me back down the drive and through the gate. I traced what I assumed to be Ronnie's shoe prints through the sand and gravel on the path that led behind The Tea Shoppe and to one of the other secluded properties. I stopped at the gate that barred the driveway. I closed my eyes again, pulling my magic back. My vision cleared when I looked around again. I could see the disturbed dirt on the other side of the gate. If I had to guess, Ronnie had jumped the barrier in the hope of finding some vibrant roses for his wife.

Romantic, but foolish and he had the cuts to prove it.

I could hear a low voice grumbling nearby and spotted an older man in a hat bent over the rose-bushes. I could see where Ronnie had clipped them, likely with a pocketknife. The stems left behind were sheared at an angle. Gardening scissors wouldn't have made a cut like that. The gardener looked up and caught me watching him.

I pocketed the leaf once more and took a step back. "Sorry, didn't mean to disturb you. I'm just staying across the way," I called.

"Well, better not have been you who destroyed Mistress Lorelei's roses," he replied.

"No, sir. Can they be salvaged?" I reached out with my powers and was relieved to know the damage wasn't insurmountable. It would take the plant time, but it would recover.

He gave a grunt. "So long as no one else comes traipsing through."

I offered an awkward wave before I retreated to the mansion across the way. I found Maggie sitting at one of the long tables in the kitchen. Ronnie was nowhere in sight. Remnants of adhesive bandages were scattered on the counter and the antiseptic hadn't been stowed away yet.

"Want to tell me what was really going on?" Maggie didn't look up from her pancakes.

"I don't know what you mean," I answered as I found a fork and snagged a bite from her plate.

"Those cuts looked like they came from thorns."

"That's because they did. He was trying to impress his new bride ... snuck across the way and pilfered some roses from the neighbors."

"He told you that?"

"Not exactly. I caught him coming back with the roses in hand. And then, I sort of ... retraced his steps."

"With magic."

"I didn't intend to Maggie. But I felt their pain when he cut them. It felt like they were screaming out. I thought my head would explode." I pressed a finger to the side of my head as if I could still feel the discomfort. "I just needed to know what happened." I hung my head. "Look, I know we promised no magic this weekend. And I swear, that's all I'll do."

She looked at me with her brow furrowed for a moment before she sighed and leaned in to plant a syrupy kiss on my lips. "I forgive you. I know how hard it is to turn off that instinct once it's firmly implanted within you."

"I don't think you could have fit more plant metaphors in that sentence if you tried," I teased.

She laughed and bumped my shoulder. "Come on, let's see what sort of non-magical trouble we can get up to."

3

Despite the thorny start to our morning, the rest of the day turned into a lovely time. We strolled along the shore for a while before retreating to the manor around lunch time. Ronnie and Mindy hadn't come down yet. However, the older couple sat in two wicker chairs on the back patio as I carried out a pitcher of fresh-squeezed lemonade I'd found in one of the fridges. Maggie followed me out with four glasses and set them on the glass table on the patio.

"So, where are you two from?" Maggie asked, breaking the uncomfortable silence.

"Vacationing from Maine," the man replied, reaching for a glass and the pitcher. "We've come down to the island for years. What about you two?"

"First holiday together," I blurted before Maggie could answer.

"I remember going on trips with my friends back in college," the man said as he poured lemonade into the glass and passed it to the woman who remained silent.

Color warmed Maggie's cheeks at his words. She made a point of stepping over and wrapping her arm firmly around my waist. "We're a couple actually."

"Oh, I ... I didn't mean any offense," the man sputtered.

"It's fine, no reason you should have known," I said, forcing a tight-lipped smile. "I didn't realize that the owners have been renting out the place for so long." I prayed a change of subject would ease the tension.

The woman turned her glass between her fingers, studying the bits of lemon seeds that had made it into her drink. "We are friends with the owners. We didn't realize they wouldn't be here when we came down this summer."

"I can imagine it would be quite lovely here with friends," I said gently. "I'm sorry they weren't able to be here with you this time."

She gave a heavy sigh. "Things are changing so much these days, it's hard to keep up."

The man patted her knee affectionately. "As I keep telling Terry, we aren't going to be left behind."

"My husband, the eternal optimist," Terry said with the ghost of a smile on her lips. "Sorry we've not been very friendly. We just aren't used to other people in the house and the rest of our company has been ... vigorous."

"You remember what we were like as newly-weds," her husband chuckled.

Terry's cheeks burned beet red. "Bernard, hush."

The pressure from Maggie's hand on my waist slackened as the tension broke between our group. "You probably know all the not-so-obvious places to go on the island. Any suggestions of where we ought to head before we go back tomorrow?" I addressed Terry.

"There's a nice little cove out that way. It's secluded. There used to be some pretty sea glass that would wash up there."

I turned to Maggie. "Fancy a picnic lunch tomorrow before we go home?"

"It's a date," she replied and kissed my cheek.

We shared our lemonade with Bernard and Terry as a balmy breeze worked its way through the patio. After a while, they retreated inside, leaving Maggie and I alone. I took up Bernard's seat and

Maggie settled into Terry's. I studied my girlfriend as she took a long pull from her lemonade glass.

"What's on your mind?" I probed.

She set the glass down and turned in the chair to face me. "Just thinking that we haven't really had a normal relationship."

"What do you mean?"

"Darcy, our first attempt at a date ended with murder. Our last big outing, did, too."

"Nothing bad has happened this time," I protested.

Her jaw worked and I could imagine her forming the word 'yet.'

"I swear, I don't go looking for trouble, if that's what you're thinking."

She reached over and squeezed my hand. "Of course, I don't think that. And I love that you're curious and smart and dedicated to finding out the truth. I just wish sometimes we could have a run-of-the-mill date. No dire straits, no magic. Like our first official date."

I smiled at the memory. Nearly six months ago, we'd done an Escape Room. No magic. No drama. It had been perfect and had cemented for me just how wonderful Maggie was.

"I promise, tomorrow's picnic will be magic and

drama-free," I vowed, sending up a silent request to the universe to make it so.

Dinner had been a pleasant affair. Ronnie and Mindy finally joined us and with the ice broken with Bernard and Terry, we'd shared a night of conversation and delicious food. Maybe the camaraderie had chased away the bad dreams, because I slept soundly that night. I woke to find Maggie already out of bed and dressed.

"Morning," I greeted, kicking aside the sheets and blankets.

"Morning," she replied and pulled me to my feet. "Thought I would make you breakfast in bed," she said, sounding only vaguely disappointed her plans had been foiled.

"And here I was thinking I was going to cook for you," I answered.

I washed up and dressed before we headed down to the kitchen. Mindy stood in front of the fridge, door ajar as she stared off into space. Ronnie was nowhere to be seen.

"You, okay?" I prompted, easing the fridge closed. "You're letting all the cold out."

She blinked and looked at me. I could see her lower lids were red rimmed from crying. "Ronnie's gone."

"Gone? What do you mean?"

"I woke up this morning and he wasn't there."

"Well, he was up early yesterday when I ran into him," I said. "He's probably off trying to find you something exotic to have for breakfast."

"I can't shake this feeling," she murmured and wandered off, leaving Maggie and I in the industrial space.

"Don't get involved," Maggie hissed as she set about pulling together the fixings for omelettes.

"I just told her what I knew," I protested. But it did make me wonder what Ronnie might be up to. Surely, he hadn't been foolish enough to sneak back across the road for more flowers.

I did my best to put the newlyweds out of my head as I set to packing food for our picnic. My culinary skills paled in comparison to either Maggie or Tania, but I could make a decent sandwich. I even found the ingredients for a simple fruit salad and some pasta.

Before long, the sun was high in the sky, and we wound our way through the foliage behind the manor to the cove Terry had mentioned. It was quiet and the water was a crystalline blue that looked impossible given the rest of the ocean around us. Maggie spread out a blanket she'd pilfered from the manor, and we settled side by side. I kicked off my shoes and dipped my toes into the shallow waters. I could feel tiny tendrils of seaweed and kale tickling the bottoms of my feet.

"Look at you being brave," Maggie teased as she took a bite of the pasta.

"This I don't mind. Open water is what still freaks me out," I retorted.

She held up her plate, using her fork to point at the food. "This is really good."

"Thanks. It's my mum's recipe." A pang of sadness tightened my chest for a moment.

It had been so long since I'd thought about my parents. The memory of us making it together hit harder than I would have anticipated.

"I know you two have a complicated relationship, but one day I am going to need to thank her for this."

"That better not be the only thing you're thanking her for," I laughed.

"Oh, I'm sure I could find other things," she replied, grabbing my hand, and kissing the back of my knuckles.

"You flirt," I chided.

"I can't help it."

A broad grin spread across my lips as I took in the beautiful surroundings—my girlfriend included—letting my worries and fears melt away. Not everything in my life had to be so dire. I could enjoy the simple moments with the people I cared about. And I was looking forward to telling Beau that he'd been worrying over nothing.

Setting my now-empty plate aside, I stood and approached the pool properly. I knelt in the soft sand as I studied the water. I could see the tiny plants that had taken notice of me before. Except I'd promised Maggie no magic, and I meant it.

"Sorry," I whispered.

The sun shifted, reflecting off the surface and I spotted something glinting at the bottom of the pool. I reached into the water and pulled out a piece of smooth almost rust colored sea glass.

"Terry was right. There is sea glass here," I called to Maggie.

I held it up, letting the light catch in it and I caught the reflection of something moving behind me. I turned, dropping the piece onto the sand as I did so. Ronnie stood just off to Maggie's right, looking bleary-eyed and rubbing at the nape of his neck.

"Woah, mate, you don't look well," I said, rushing forward as he took a shaky step toward me.

"How'd I get here?" His words came out slow, as if he was remembering how to talk after not using his voice in a long while.

"What's the last thing you remember?" Maggie prompted, offering him some water and half of her sandwich.

"Mindy and I had a drink last night I think ... then, I was here?"

"Come on, let's get you back to the manor. You look like you need to lie down," I said.

Maggie made sure he ate the food she'd shoved into his hand and drank while I picked up our picnic.

So much for drama-free.

Getting him to ascend the two curving staircases took some doing with both Maggie and I supporting his weight as we dragged him to his room. The longer it took, the less he appeared to be able to hold up his own weight. At the top of the second flight, Mindy appeared, eyes wide.

"Ronnie!" she exclaimed and raced toward him.

"Easy, he's a bit out of it," I warned.

"Let's get him laying down and we'll check his vitals," Maggie explained, slipping into healer mode.

We settled him against the pillows, and it was then that I noticed just how pale the man's face had become. Maggie set about checking his pulse and heart rate.

"His heart rate is elevated, and he feels feverish. I'm not sure where he's been all morning, but he looks dehydrated. We can try to get him to drink and eat, but honestly, the best bet is to get him to a hospital for a full exam."

"But the boat doesn't come until tonight," Mindy whimpered.

I pulled Maggie aside. "Do you think we could keep him hydrated until then? Or should we call Chief Hayes?"

"Never thought I'd hear you suggest we call Rick," Maggie murmured. "I'm going to talk to Corinne and see if she can arrange something for earlier."

"What can I do to help?"

"Just keep trying to get him to drink. Maybe use some cool cloths to try and bring the fever down."

Mindy sat on Ronnie's right, stroking his hair and squeezing his hand. "It's going to be okay, babe," she said, fighting back tears.

"I'm going to get some cool cloths. I'll be right back." I left the newlyweds in the room and raced to the bathroom; grateful it was unoccupied. I found as many face cloths as I could carry and ran them under cold water. The front of my shirt turned damp as I carried them back to the room and pressed them to Ronnie's forehead and bare arms.

He gave a soft moan and turned away as I tried to wipe his left cheek. I spotted something that looked angry and red on the side of his neck. I didn't get a chance to examine it further before Maggie returned with Corinne hot on her heels.

"I've got a charter coming now. It should arrive in about twenty minutes," Corinne said.

"What do I do?" Mindy asked, looking at the rest of us with a helpless expression.

To my surprise, Corinne stepped up. "I'll help you pack, while these lovely ladies look after him."

"Someone should go with them on the boat," Maggie said.

"Doesn't make sense for just one of us to go," I pointed out. "I'll go pack our things."

This wasn't how I'd envisioned ending our weekend getaway, but I couldn't deny that helping Ronnie was the right thing to do. Collecting our belongings took hardly any time at all as I tossed dirty clothes into one bag and toiletries into the other. By the time I made it to the first floor, Mindy and Maggie were already there supporting Ronnie. He looked awful with his head lolling to one side. I hoped he would make it through the boat ride.

True to her word, Corinne's charter boat appeared just as we reached the shore. The captain lowered the gangplank and our quartet climbed aboard. We laid Ronnie down on one of the benches below deck, his head propped in Mindy's lap. Her hands shook as the boat cut through choppy water back to Brookhaven.

I found myself gripping Maggie's hand so tight my knuckles turned white until we'd reached the boardwalk in town. I was first up on deck, and I realized we didn't have a way to get Ronnie to the hospital without walking. I thought about calling Tania, but her VW was much too small to cram four people into, one of them severely ill.

Just as Maggie, Mindy, and Ronnie appeared on deck, a sedan pulled up on the street and the driver rolled down the window. Ginny looked out at me. "Maggie said you needed a ride."

"You're a life saver," I called and opened the back door, so that the other two women could ease Ronnie in. I climbed into the front passenger seat.

"Not that I'm encouraging you to break the law,

but you might want to step on it," Maggie called from the back seat.

Ginny flashed me a toothy grin. "Lucky for us, I have an in with the police."

She pressed the gas pedal to the floor and the sedan shot forward, zipping past the row of shops on Main Street and pulling up to the Emergency entrance at the hospital.

I was already out of the car and easing Maggie's door open when I heard Mindy let out a strangled sound. I met Maggie's gaze, and I instantly knew something was wrong.

"We need to lay him flat," Maggie said, her tone sharp and firm.

We managed to get him onto the ground and out of Ginny's car before Maggie probed his neck and felt his wrist. She hung her head, and I heard her fight back a sob of her own. When she looked up at me again, her jaw was set. "We were too late. He's dead."

4

Mindy recovered her wits first after Maggie's statement. She shook her head, tugging Ronnie's arms as if to rouse him.

"No, he's just passed out," she shouted.

"I'm sorry, but I don't feel a pulse," Maggie said just as the automatic doors to the Emergency Room slid open and a scrub-clad doctor and nurse appeared guiding a gurney.

"What happened?" the doctor—a woman with long dark hair twisted up into a knot at the base of her skull—called out.

"He presented as dehydrated a couple of hours ago. Rapid heart rate, fever," Maggie answered. "Now I can't get a pulse.

The doctor gestured to the nurse once they'd gotten Ronnie's body on the gurney and the nurse straddled Ronnie's torso, administering chest compressions. Mindy scurried after them as they raced into the hospital proper.

"They'll revive him, right?" I asked Maggie, the smallest hint of hope coloring my tone.

"I don't know. His symptoms had such a rapid onset, and he went downhill so fast."

"If he was exposed to something on the island, Rick will need to know," Ginny said from the driver seat of the sedan.

"But we don't even know what we'd be reporting," I answered.

"That's for them to figure out. You two did your Good Samaritan duty," Ginny answered. The car gave a beep and the trunk opened. I retrieved the bags from the back and set them on the sidewalk as Ginny pulled away.

"I agree with you. Until we know he's actually dead, I don't think we have enough information to report anything," Maggie said. I held out my hand to pull her up.

"Do you think it could have been a reaction to getting bitten by something?"

"What makes you think that?"

"I thought I noticed something red on his neck. Maybe a bug bite or an animal stung him? It could have happened when he was wandering out near the ocean and encountered something. He could have just had a reaction to it."

"Possibly." Maggie glanced toward the automatic doors.

I took her hand in mine and urged her toward it. "Come on, I'm sure Mindy could use the moral support."

It wasn't hard to find her. She sat outside one of the curtained off bays. I couldn't hear much from beyond the barrier. That wasn't a good sign. I touched the woman's shoulder and she jumped, flinching at my touch.

"Sorry, didn't mean to startle you. We just wanted to let you know that we're here for you."

"Th-Thanks."

"What did the doctor say?" Maggie prompted softly, bending down to Mindy's eye line.

"They took him away, but I just have this terrible feeling," she answered, devolving in sobs.

I patted the girl's shoulder, feeling uncomfortable giving her a hug. Maggie appeared to have no qualms about it and pulled Mindy into a tight embrace.

Shoes squeaked on the tile flooring and Maggie turned to see the doctor who'd come out to meet us approaching. The somber expression on her face didn't bode well.

"Can I see Ronnie? Where is he?" The words spilled out of Mindy's mouth as she pulled herself from Maggie's embrace and stood up.

"I'm very sorry, but we were unable to revive your husband," the doctor replied.

"N-no. That's not right. He was fine yesterday. You need to try harder," Mindy demanded, beginning to pace.

"I wish there was more that we could do, but he was too weak." The doctor made a tentative grab for Mindy's arm. "But you can come through and see him if you want."

Mindy's sobbing resumed, but she nodded in between hitches of breath, allowing the doctor to guide her deeper into the hospital. Before she left, the doctor pivoted and looked to the charge nurse seated at the central desk.

"Do me a favor, call the authorities. It looks like this might have been foul play."

"Yes, doctor," the charge nurse responded, phone already out of the cradle.

As I stood there in the bright, sterile environment, my mind began to whir with thoughts. What had led the doctor to suspect foul play? Did she think Mindy might be involved?

"Hi, Vinnie, it's April. We've got another one. You're going to need to come down to the hospital."

Another one?

The look on Maggie's face suggested she shared my thoughts and we both moved to stand opposite April at the nurse's desk. She set the phone back in its cradle and looked up at us.

"I shouldn't say anything, but there's been some strange deaths lately with similar symptoms to your guy."

I could feel my desire to unearth the truth growing. Though I didn't owe Mindy anything. I'd already done what I could to get her husband help. And yet, I couldn't deny that my curiosity was piqued.

"Darcy..." Maggie began, but I cut her off.

"I know. Don't get involved."

About five minutes later, the doors to the ER swished open and Vinnie walked in. He made eye contact with me, but moved to address Nurse April. "Want to point me in the right direction?"

"I'll page Dr. Fuentes to come out and explain. But these two were with the deceased and his wife."

Vinnie glanced over his shoulder at us and sighed. "Thanks."

"And here I thought we were going to have a record. Almost made it six months without your name showing up in a file," Vinnie said to me. I'd have expected that sort of annoyance from Chief Hayes, not his deputy. He was generally more affable.

"Would you believe me if I said I was just having a weekend away with Maggie and we happened to be sharing a manor with Ronnie and his wife?"

"Ronnie?"

"The deceased," Maggie prompted.

"Right." Vinnie opened his notepad and clicked the point of his pen out. "So, why don't you fill me in on what you know?"

"We don't know much," I began, taking the lead. "We'd gone to this mansion on Haven Island. The owners were renting out rooms for the weekend. It was us, Ronnie and his wife Mindy, and then an older couple, Bernard and Terry."

"Did you all spend much time together?"

"Not really. We had dinner last night and we chatted with Terry and Bernard a bit yesterday afternoon. But Ronnie and Mindy kept to themselves," I answered.

"They were on their honeymoon," Maggie supplied.

Vinnie gave an understanding head nod. "How'd they seem to you during the weekend?"

"Fine, at first. Ronnie was all excited to make breakfast for her. Yesterday morning, I caught him sneaking back with some roses he'd taken from the neighbor's garden," I continued. Vinnie's eyebrows raised with interest at my statement. "Oh, I don't think the neighbors offed him for taking a few flowers. Honestly, I don't even know that they realized ... other than the gardener."

"Ronnie earned some cuts and scratches from his escapade," Maggie interjected. "But I patched him up and he seemed perfectly fine at dinner."

"But then he went missing this morning and came wandering through a cove at the back of the property a little after noontime," I added. "We were having a picnic and he just showed up. He looked really out of it. He couldn't remember where he'd been or how he'd gotten there."

"He was feverish and had a rapid heart rate,"

Maggie noted. "But Dr. Fuentes said he was too weak. He arrested right when we arrived here."

"And did you notice anything that might account for his sudden change in condition?"

Subconsciously, I brushed my fingers against the side of my neck. "I noticed some sort of bruising or bite on his neck. Though I didn't notice too many bugs on the island, but maybe he got bit and had a reaction?"

"Something bit him," Vinnie muttered under his breath. "Maybe. I'm sure the lab will do a full work up. Uh, did you administer any other aid to him prior to his death?"

"We gave him some water, tried to cool him off with some cool cloths. But we got a charter as soon as we could to get him back to the mainland," Maggie answered.

"Right. Okay." He scribbled something down on his pad I couldn't read. "And you're sure he was alone when you found him?"

"We didn't see anyone else around when we were bringing him back inside," I offered.

Vinnie cast a glance around the empty space. Nurse April had disappeared; possibly to find Dr. Fuentes in person. Satisfied we wouldn't be overheard, Vinnie whispered, "Did you happen to notice if he had all of his vital organs?"

"Excuse me?" I blurted.

"Was it obvious if he was missing anything you might need to keep on living?"

"Not that I noticed," I answered and looked to Maggie who shook her head.

"I didn't notice anything either. He had trouble bearing his own weight by the time we got him back to the manor. But I didn't notice that he was particularly sensitive anywhere. And he wasn't bleeding that I could see," Maggie said in one long breath.

"I heard Nurse April tell you that Ronnie was 'another one,'" I probed. "What did that mean?"

Vinnie hung his head. "You know I can't talk about an ongoing case, Darcy."

Before I could ask more questions, Nurse April and Dr. Fuentes appeared. The doctor gestured for Vinnie to follow her, no doubt to inspect Ronnie's body and take Mindy's statement. Maggie and I were left standing in the Emergency Room with no real reason to be there anymore.

"We should go," Maggie said.

"Right, yeah. Did you want to come back to the B&B with me or ..." I trailed off. I couldn't put my finger on why exactly, but I didn't want Maggie to go back to her apartment. Maybe it was the trauma of seeing Mindy lose the man she loved, but I didn't want to be that far from my girlfriend.

"The B&B sounds like a good idea."

The way she gripped my hand and held tight to my arm as we left the hospital told me she felt that same need to be close to those she cared about. We'd barely made it up the driveway of the B&B before Tania opened the front door and stepped onto the porch.

"What's happened?"

For a split second I forgot she couldn't actually see the future. "A man's dead. The police are investigating," I said, the words tumbling out of my mouth as I walked up the steps.

"One of the vacationers at the mansion," Maggie added. "Young guy. He deteriorated so fast."

"It sounds like there's some sort of active investigation. The man that died, Ronnie might not be the first person," I added as I passed my landlady in the doorway and scanned the banister, hoping to catch a glimpse of Beau hiding in plain sight. I didn't spot him and a quick swipe of the wood with my hand revealed he wasn't on the first floor.

"Where's Beau?"

"Upstairs I expect. He's been nestled on your pillow since you left."

"Darcy, what are you thinking?" Maggie called up the stairs after me.

I was thinking that my chameleon companion had warned me that something was hunting in our town. And now a man was dead from unusual causes. I ignored the thunder of footsteps on the stairs behind me as I entered my bedroom. I settled on the edge of the bed and carefully ran my hand across the pillow, feeling the chameleon's rough scales beneath my fingers. With a shimmer, Beau changed his coloring, so he no longer blended in with the pillowcase and opened both eyes.

'Home now. Home safe.'

"I might be, but a man is dead, Beau. You were trying to warn me before I left that something was hunting. Do you know what it is?"

Beau blinked a few times before I heard, *'Danger to all.'*

"What sort of danger? Ronnie didn't deserve to die. If you know something, please tell me," I begged.

"Even if he could tell you, how do you think you're going to pass that on to the police?" Maggie challenged.

"Chief Hayes knows I'm a witch. He's seen me use my magic more than once. I'd tell him I found out that way. I doubt he'd much care how I came by the information if it helped him solve a case."

"Rick wouldn't be pleased with you inserting yourself in another one of his cases," Tania added.

I looked at Maggie. "You can't tell me you didn't pick up on Vinnie's stress. I don't know how long this has been going on, but clearly, they're stumped. And I think we can all agree that Chief Hayes is less than pleasant when he's got a case that isn't solved."

"Okay, fine," Maggie sighed. "If we can figure out what it is, we should pass it along as anonymously as possible."

"So that's settled," I said with a nod.

"But you're the only one who saw what was on his neck. I didn't catch it at all." Maggie's voice cracked on the last few words.

"You were dealing with his fever and a clingy wife. It's understandable," I consoled her. "And I wasn't even sure of what I saw at first."

"Perhaps Beau needs more information to go on to explain what he was warning you about?" Tania interjected before Maggie could spiral into self-doubt.

I looked down at the reptile on my pillow. "Is this danger something you've seen personally? Can you describe it?"

'Only sense it. Hunting, hurting. Killing.'

The last word sent shivers down my spine. I closed my eyes, trying to recall what I'd noticed on Ronnie's neck. It had definitely been red and the skin irritated. Had the skin been broken? Maybe? An image flashed through my brain of two neat puncture wounds right over Ronnie's jugular vein. I tried to push it away, but my gut told me that was in fact what I'd seen. *But it couldn't be that.*

"It looked like a couple of punctures. So, maybe not bug bites like I'd first thought. Maybe something else bit him," I said. I still couldn't bring myself to say the word that my mind conjured. Witches and ghosts existed, sure, but there had to be a line somewhere. In this moment, my mind wouldn't let me accept that I might be about to cross it.

I wanted to suggest something like a stray dog or a cat, but those sorts of bites would have left more wounds than just two. I watched Maggie work through the scenario too. She reached out and touched my neck. "Were they about here?"

I nodded. "Might have been."

"Two punctures directly in the neck?" Tania asked, color draining from her cheeks.

"Like I said, it could have been. I'm not entirely sure of what I saw."

Tania crossed herself and muttered under her breath, no doubt trying to ward off some unseen evil.

"You can't be suggesting what I think you're suggesting," I protested.

Maggie and Tania shared a look and then nodded in unison.

Beau blinked up at me and his head bobbed as if to agree with them. *'Vampire.'*

5

I burst out laughing. I looked from Beau, to Tania, to Maggie, and then back. Both women looked completely serious, if a bit nervous. This had to be some sort of joke.

"You're telling me vampires are a real thing?"

"Yes ... They're exceedingly rare, but there have been some reports throughout the years," Tania answered softly.

"But we were on a sunny beach in the middle of the day." From what I knew about vampire lore, they couldn't go out in sunlight. Or was that just tales spun by the real thing to help them hide amongst society?"

"To be honest, I've never encountered anything

that might even come close to the stories, but I know they are real," Maggie replied.

A vampire would explain the punctures on Ronnie's neck and why he felt so weak. If someone had drunk his blood, then he'd certainly have far less of it in him. "Wait. Do they eat organs?"

"Not that I know of. Why do you ask?" Tania responded.

Maggie's eyes went wide. "Because Vinnie said Ronnie wasn't the first person to show up with these sorts of symptoms. He may have let slip that possibly others had lost organs."

I rubbed at my temples. "But why would they take people's organs if they don't need them?"

I barely repressed a shiver that raced down my spine at the thought of what Ronnie might have lost and we hadn't noticed. "I still need to tell Chief Hayes what I saw. It could be helpful."

"I think you two ought to get cleaned up first," Tania said with a note of finality.

I insisted Maggie shower first. I laid on my bed and Beau nestled against my shoulder as I tried not to spiral.

I failed.

I mentally cataloged all the bizarre behaviors Ronnie had exhibited upon meeting him. He hadn't seemed the type to act recklessly. Yet he'd snuck out and stolen flowers for his new bride, Mindy. And he'd been careless enough to not wear gardening gloves, so he'd come back with thorn scratches and cuts. Had that been on purpose? Had something lured him there in order to get his blood?

Could he have gone wandering off again early this morning before Mindy woke? Was that when the ... vampire had bitten him? If in fact he had been bitten, why had his attacker allowed him to leave again? If I were a blood-sucking villain, I wouldn't want my victims to be able to identify me.

Well, I wasn't going to get anywhere just sitting here, spinning theories in my mind. Thankfully, Maggie appeared in the doorway at that moment.

"Bathroom's yours. I'm going to head back to my apartment and drop my stuff off."

"Will you come with me when I go to the police station?"

She gave me a half smile. "Sure."

I pushed myself off the bed and closed the distance between us, giving her a quick kiss. "Thank you. And again, I'm sorry this ruined our weekend."

She brushed a curl off my cheek. "As far as I know, you didn't summon a vampire, so I'm pretty sure none of this was your fault."

"I just feel bad," I murmured.

"And I appreciate that. But I promise you have nothing to feel bad about. I'll meet you at the station."

I nodded and she stepped in from the doorway, letting me pass. I padded down the hall to the bathroom. When we had guests, I kept my toiletries in a caddy. However, since we were essentially vacant right now, I was able to store my things in the bathroom.

I picked up on the eucalyptus-scented body wash Maggie had clearly just used and I let the smell ease my anxiety. Before long, I was immersed in the shower's steam and the soothing fragrance. When I emerged, I could almost pretend nothing strange had happened. Almost.

I dressed and headed back downstairs. I found Tania standing by the front door, a cup of Maggie's special chamomile tea in hand. She held it out to me.

"Thanks." It wasn't exactly what I envisioned to fortify my nerves at voluntarily speaking to Rick Hayes, but if it kept my nerves in check, I'd take it.

"I am so sorry you had to watch a man die today," Tania said, touching my elbow as I brought the mug up to my lips.

"Not how I expected my mini holiday to end." I drained the mug's contents in a few quick gulps. "My head's just full of questions. I know it's none of my business, but I can't help feeling as though I'm supposed to do … I don't know … something."

"You have great compassion for those around you and you don't like to see them hurting. That could manifest as an intense curiosity …" Tania answered, trailing off as if she'd intended to say more.

"But this time, it really isn't my business. Rick and Vinnie have it handled. Besides, if Ronnie was really killed by a vampire, I am horribly ill-equipped to deal with that."

Sure, I'd contended with a couple of witches with malintent. But at least I had a basic grasp on how their powers worked. I didn't know the first thing about going up against a vampire. I knew about the things spouted in popular culture and myths. Though even what I'd learned in the last year about magic diverged drastically from how the media portrays witches.

"You are right to take what you know to the police. Let's hope that's enough to give them a clue they didn't have before."

I nodded and turned toward the kitchen, intent

on rinsing the mug and setting it down to dry. Tania plucked it from my fingers and made a shooing motion. Well, I had my marching orders. Time to see a policeman about a vampire.

TRUE TO HER WORD, MAGGIE WAITED FOR ME OUTSIDE the police station. Without a word, she looped her arm through mine, and together we walked in through the automatic doors. As we passed inside, I couldn't help recalling all the times I'd snuck into the station under the cover of Beau's magic to go snooping where I technically didn't belong. I'd been fortunate those times not to get caught. But the law of averages suggested one day my luck would run out.

Vinnie was nowhere to be seen. There'd been rumblings around town of Chief Hayes hiring on a few more officers since crime had risen in the last year, but that hadn't happened yet. Something about the budget. I might be a member of this community now, but I didn't feel comfortable getting involved in that sort of drama.

Unlike the many times I'd been here, both with the chief's knowledge and without, there was a rolling board set up just outside the chief's office with pictures of several people. At first, they appeared to have nothing in common. However, the notes scrawled underneath in dry erase marker suggested they'd all been found dead. Most had been missing organs. And not just one or two, but multiple.

That sent a shiver of disgust down my spine, and I swallowed back bile rising in my throat. Maggie stopped walking, halting my forward momentum to keep me away from the board.

"We're just here to tell him what you saw on Ronnie," she reminded me in a whisper.

"I know," I said. But I couldn't take my eyes off the people on the board.

I felt silly standing there, waiting for someone to notice us. I was a little surprised no one had heard the doors open for us, but we stood in the main area alone. I unlinked my arm from Maggie's and took a tentative step toward Chief Hayes' office. The door was open enough for me to see that no one was in there. Yet, the lights were on, and I could see a partially drunk cup of coffee on the desk.

"Can I help you with something?" Chief Hayes' voice came from behind me.

I'm not proud of the fact I squealed in surprise as

I spun to face him. Like always, he stood in his uniform with his overly intense brown gaze focused on me. Light reflected in his eyes making them take on an amber sheen.

"I had some information I thought you should know about the man who died today."

"Ronnie Swanson," Chief Hayes noted.

I glanced at Maggie. "I didn't know his last name. But yeah, him."

"You gave Vinnie statements at the scene, isn't that, right?"

"We did, Rick, but Darcy remembered something after we got back to Tania's. It's important," Maggie interjected.

The chief let out a sigh and gestured for us to enter his office. I settled in one of the chairs opposite him, still feeling uneasy about his sudden appearance. Maggie sat beside me, and we waited for Rick to join us. He sat, picked up his mug, glanced at its contents, and set it back down.

"What did you need to tell me, Miss Ingram?"

"I'm sure you've noticed that strange things happen in this town," I began.

"Yes, we have an inordinate amount of dead bodies popping up in my jurisdiction. What's your point?"

"Well, I mean, you've seen things that some people might think are impossible."

"Like a woman who can control plants," he answered with an arched brow.

"Uh, yes ... like that. Anyway, the thing I remember was Ronnie had some marks on his neck. Initially I dismissed it as a bug bite or something. But the more I thought about it, the more I recalled there wasn't just one mark. There were two."

"Anything else?"

"They looked more like punctures than raised like a mosquito or bug bite might do. But I think something bit him. Maybe it made him sick."

Chief Hayes studied me then turned his attention to Maggie. "You're in the medical field and you were with her. What did you see?"

"Honestly, not much. I was trying to keep him hydrated and bring his fever down. But I believe Darcy."

"Chief, I know it's not my business, but what exactly do you think is going on here?" I couldn't stop myself from asking the question.

"You're right, it's not your business."

"You aren't exactly hiding an ongoing investigation out there." Maggie hooked a thumb over her shoulder. "If people are in danger, they ought to know."

The chief's jaw tightened, and he looked even more annoyed than usual when I was in his presence. "We don't know if they're connected, but we have had a string of strange deaths. Bodies missing a lot of blood and some vital organs."

"Did they have bite marks?" I blurted.

He glared at me.

"If Ronnie's death is somehow related, then it might give you more information since whatever happened to him occurred over on Haven Island."

"Let's assume for a moment, that you were correct, and something bit Ronnie. What exactly do you think did it?" The look in his eyes dared me to speak the word aloud.

"Given that he was weak, pale, and there were two punctures, it looked like maybe a ... a vampire." The last word came out in a whisper.

"What was that?"

"Vampire," I repeated, more forceful this time. "I know it sounds mental. But in a town full of witches, isn't it possible?"

I expected him to laugh me out of his office. Instead, he sat there, contemplating my statement "It isn't the craziest theory I've heard."

"It's not?"

"We'll look into every potential avenue. But right now, if you don't mind, I have a grieving widow to interview."

"You should speak to Bernard and Terry," I said as Maggie and I stood to leave.

"Who?"

"The other couple at the mansion for the weekend. They might have seen something we didn't."

If there really was something hunting the island's shores, I didn't want them to be its next victim. Or maybe they'd have some sense of whether anything new had come to the island recently.

"I'll take it under advisement."

"Thank you," I said before heading for the door.

"One last thing," he called.

I pivoted on my heel to face him. "Yes?"

"Can you confirm which side of his neck the bitemarks were on?"

"Right side," I answered.

He gave me a dismissive nod, jotting down the information on a pad on his desk. I resisted the urge to stop by the board in the bullpen and see whether the other people who had turned up dead had bite marks on the right side of their necks, too. Even if Ronnie was part of this same string of deaths, my involvement ended at the hospital, where I'd tried to get him help. Sadly, I'd just been too late. I had no more reason to get involved.

Just keep telling yourself that, Darcy.

Relief washed over me the moment we stepped into the late morning sunlight. The breeze tugged at the loose curls around my face, and I sighed. Rick hadn't thought I was absolutely mental. Clearly, more people in this town believed in the supernatural than I'd first assumed. Maybe I didn't need to hide my own abilities quite as much as I did. Yes, I could be more open with my magic here than back in England. Still, I didn't go around showing off that I could make roses bloom with just a whisper. But maybe I shouldn't be afraid of doing that. People might be even more accepting of me than I'd realized.

As it stood now, I didn't know what was real and what was fiction. But there might be one person in town who could tell me what I wanted to know or at least point me in the right direction to figure it out.

"Fancy an early lunch?" I asked Maggie.

Maggie glanced at me with skepticism. "Why do I get the feeling you've got something else in mind other than a nice meal?"

I didn't doubt we'd get a nice meal out of this,

but it wasn't my main objective. "Because you know me so well," I replied with a smirk.

"Want to give me a hint about what we're doing?"

I turned, so I was facing my girlfriend as I started walking backwards. I took both her hands in mine, trusting that she wouldn't let me walk into anything or anyone. Not that the sidewalk was particularly busy right in front of the police station on a Sunday morning. "I've just learned that creatures I thought were fiction are real and could be roaming around my home. I want to learn everything I can about them. The *truth* about them."

Maggie gave me an understanding nod as I emphasized the word 'truth.' I spun back around, still keeping hold of one of her hands. We made our way up Main Street to the only decent place in this town to get a cup of coffee and to find out the town's supernatural secrets.

6

Ginny's was surprisingly empty. Normally I would expect the after-church lunch crowd to have filled up the booths. But only a handful of people sat eating lunch. Thankfully, even though the patrons were scarce, the café's owner sat at her usual spot at the counter, nursing an oversized cup of coffee. I wasted no time sitting down beside her and Maggie settled in on my right.

"I hope you don't need me to drive you anywhere else. I've done my good deed for the day," Ginny said, sounding tired.

"No. And thanks again for what you did," I replied, forcing myself to study the menu in front of me. I couldn't just launch into a litany of questions about vampires.

"That poor woman. She looked so heartbroken," Ginny noted.

"They'd just gotten married and were on their honeymoon," I said, offering up the little I knew about the couple.

"What can I get you?" one of the servers—a young man with shaggy red hair—said from the opposite side of the counter.

"I'll just have a Caesar salad," Maggie replied.

"Same," I said, pushing the menu away. It wasn't the most filling of meals, but if I was about to be discussing blood and the undead, I didn't want a lot in my stomach.

The server picked up the menus, cast a nervous look at Ginny and darted through the door to the kitchen. I didn't recall seeing him before and I'd started to consider myself one of Ginny's regulars, even if she wouldn't agree.

"That's Frankie, he's new. Don't mind him," Ginny said, dismissing the young man. "Why are you really here, Darcy?"

"I can't just come to enjoy a nice lunch?" I quipped.

She spun on her stool and looked me point blank in the face. "Not when you deliberately sit next to me. So, what is it you want?"

"I just learned that vampires are real," I said, suddenly grateful for the lack of potential eavesdroppers.

"And you think I'm a vampire encyclopedia?"

"You know everything that goes on in this town. I figured, if vampires are a thing, you'd know about them. Or where I might look if I wanted to learn more," I answered. I felt a mild warmth spread over me as Ginny continued to stare at me.

Her magic compelled people to share the truth, so I wasn't surprised I'd told her that information. Not that I'd intended to lie to her anyway. I wasn't sure I physically could. But I didn't recall ever really feeling her magic working on me before. Logically I knew it had to have happened before, but nothing stood out. Not like this time.

Ginny took a dramatic sip from her oversized cup, as if she intended to deny my request outright. "I'm no expert, but I'll tell you what I know for certain."

The red-haired server reappeared with our salads before darting off to tend to one of the booths, hurriedly clearing the empty dishes.

"Vampires aren't like the creatures you hear about in stories. At least not entirely. They don't like the sun, but they don't turn to dust. It makes them ill. They definitely don't sleep in coffins or turn into bats either."

Ronnie's dazed demeanor came to mind. "Could they hypnotize someone?"

"It's possible. Supposedly their bite contains something that anesthetizes the victim, so they're less likely to fight back."

"How common are they? I mean, could I have walked by one and not known it at night?"

"I'd say they're less common than witches. Personally, I've never met one that I can remember, though," Ginny admitted.

That begged the question, how did she know even this much about them if she'd not spoken to one?

"How do they ... uh, happen?" Could Ronnie suddenly wake in the morgue with fangs and a thirst for blood?

"That I've never been able to figure out completely. But I'd guess it does in fact involve drinking the vampire's blood yourself."

I tried to picture Ronnie's face in my mind's eye. He'd been pale and confused, but I hadn't noticed any blood around his mouth. I let out a soft sigh, trying to convince myself I wasn't about to meet a real-life vampire.

"If I did want to learn more about them, where would I go?" Something told me I couldn't just find what I wanted from the public library.

"Look, I don't know why you're suddenly interested in vampires, but they aren't something you should go poking around about. They can be dangerous," Ginny pointed out.

"Yeah, I gathered that. But I'm just curious to learn anything I can. There's still so much I don't know about magic and the supernatural. If I'm going to be a halfway decent witch, I ought to know what else I might run across."

"Darcy, you don't need to go bumping against the darker parts of the supernatural to be a good witch," Maggie said.

"Your girlfriend's right. We keep things separate from the creatures," Ginny said.

The way she said the word creatures caught my attention. There was a hint of something like revulsion in it, but I didn't think it was levied at the unnamed supernaturals of which she now spoke.

"I appreciate you both wanting to protect me, but I need this. If I'm going to be a fully-fledged member of this town, I need to understand all of its parts, even the ugly bits."

"Fine. If you really want to know about vampires,

you should talk to Devina Coombs. She lives not far from Tyson's shop. But fair warning, she doesn't like visitors and she doesn't trust people she doesn't know."

That last part didn't surprise me. I'd encountered my fair share of people who didn't like me in Brookhaven, because they didn't know me. I counted Ginny among those who'd taken a while to warm to my presence.

"Thank you. That's all I needed," I said.

Beside me, Maggie's phone buzzed in her pocket. She pulled it out, studied the screen for a moment and sighed. "I hate to eat and run but I just got a text from Elijah. He wants me to go in for an overnight shift."

"You don't work for the hospital. You can say no," Ginny offered pointedly.

"I know. But I've been learning a lot and I'll be able to apply it at the clinic. And maybe I'll be able to save some people needing a trip to the hospital in the first place."

"Call me if you need me," I said and leaned over to give her a kiss on the cheek.

"Stay out of trouble while I'm gone," she said. Her tone was only half joking.

"I'm going to go home, have a nice nap, maybe read a book, and then go to work in the morning. Like a normal person," I called after her.

"I'm impressed," Ginny said.

"With what?" I looked at her.

"The fact you were able to just lie to her while sitting next to me. Most people can't do that."

"What? It wasn't a lie," I retorted.

"Oh, come on, Darcy. We both know the minute you walk out of here; you're going to race off to see Devina."

I couldn't deny that I was tempted to pay the woman a visit. But I wanted to know what I was walking into first. Besides, the morning's stress was starting to catch up to me again. The shower and food had helped, but I could do with some quiet time alone in a familiar space.

"I swear, I'm going home," I said and slapped a few bills on the table to pay for the meal and leave Frankie with a nice tip to hopefully ease his new hire jitters.

I left Ginny's behind, walking with purpose back to the B&B. I heard Tania moving around the kitchen, but I made my way upstairs to my room. Beau had vacated his spot on my pillow, and I curled up with it, feeling the residual bits of warmth his presence had left behind. I closed my eyes, trying to get my mind to quiet itself enough for me to sleep. But my phone buzzed with an incoming text message. I opened one eye and squinted at the screen to see a message from my cousin Piper.

> Hey, Darcy. Just wanted to check in and see how things are going.

I was still amazed that Piper wanted to be a part of my life, especially after her first encounter with me had landed her in the hospital. But she'd insisted she was grateful for having connected with me. And if I was being honest, I was pretty happy to have her in my life, too.

> Weird things are happening in town again. More people have died. Possibly vampires are involved or behind it.

Her response came almost instantly.

> You're serious? You really weren't kidding when you said bad stuff happens in that town.

Believe me, I wish I were making it up or dreaming. But it is definitely real life.

Vampires are real?

Apparently. Makes sense in a way. Magic is real. Ghosts and telepathic animals are real. Witches are real. So, why not the undead? The stories had to come from somewhere, right?

Yeah, that does make some sort of sense. What are you going to do about it?

I'm trying to leave it alone. It's not my problem. But I am curious to know more about them in general. I've got a lead I might follow.

Just stay safe.

I promise I'll be careful.

Mom is going to lose it when I tell her vampires are real.

I wasn't sure sharing it with my Aunt Audrey was the best idea. For a witch, she was pretty averse to magic and using it openly. To know vampires exist, might be a step too far.

> Try not to shock her world too much. She's not as comfortable in this world as you and I.

The three dots populated for a while then the bubble vanished. I waited for her to send something else, but nothing came.

> I ought to get some sleep. It's been a rough day. Talk soon.

I stowed my phone on the night table and rolled over, so the screen's light wouldn't lure me back to checking whether Piper sent a reply. There was always tomorrow. Outside, the sky was still a vibrant shade of blue, but I forced my eyes shut, blocking out the world.

I dreamt of Ronnie. Somehow, I knew I was dreaming, but I couldn't wake myself up. Ronnie appeared first at the cove, then the mansion where we'd stayed. His cheeks were sunken and hollow, his eyes glazed over, and sharp fangs protruded from under his upper lip. Every time I tried to run, he would appear, pale hands reached out in gnarled claws to try and catch me.

"Hello? Help!" I cried out, but no one heard me. It only served to draw him nearer.

He grabbed me around the middle, holding tight with a vice-like grip. In my dream state I registered there was no breath on my neck. In my bid to get away, I elbowed him in the ribs. He let out an 'oomph' even though he no longer needed to breathe and when I turned, I found a large red stain on his shirt. I felt my arm and my fingers came away sticky.

"This isn't real. Come on, Darcy, wake up!"

I cast about wildly searching for an exit when I spotted the door to the kitchen. Something compelled me toward it. I only hoped it would lead me to safety and the waking world. I crashed through the door ...

I landed with a painful thump on the floor, narrowly avoiding a collision with the side table. The sheets had tangled around my body, constricting my movement. Cold sweat drenched me from head to toe, making it all the more difficult to free myself from the tangled sheets and blankets. When I'd finally managed to unwind myself and got to my feet, I heard footsteps stop outside my door.

"Darcy, are you all right?" Tania called. "I heard something fall."

"Just me. Had a bad dream and managed to fall out of bed."

"How about I make you some of Maggie's tea? That might help calm things and let you get some decent rest."

"Sounds lovely. Thank you."

While she went to make the tea, I peeled off my soaked clothing. After wrapping myself in the discarded towel from earlier, I darted to the bathroom for a quick shower. I stepped out of the bathroom ten minutes later feeling less grimy to find Sam hovering in the hall, looking genuinely worried.

"What's up with you?" I prompted, retreating to my bedroom to find the promised cup of tea waiting on the side table.

"I heard we might have a fanged assailant in our midst."

"Doubt they're in the B&B. I'm not even sure they're in town. Why are you worried anyway, you're already dead?"

"Have you ever heard of a good vampire? And those guys on Buffy don't count."

I stood there, trying to think of anything even from popular lore that portrayed them as altruistic. Nothing came to mind. "Okay, probably not. But how does that affect you as a ghost? Can you sense them?" I stopped short of pointing out clearly Beau had picked up on something amiss in town.

"They just give supernaturals a bad name. And honestly, have I ever harmed more than your ego with our witty repartee?"

"No."

"Exactly. Ghosts are harmless. Sure, we'd rather not be here anymore, but that's the breaks. Those creatures choose to stay around way longer than they're meant to. It just ... It isn't right."

I could understand his point, but that didn't mean I agreed with it. If he'd never actually met a vampire, how could he say with any certainty that they'd chosen that existence. I could think of plenty of pop culture examples of vampires who had that existence forced upon them.

"Well, it isn't our problem. If there is a vampire in town, Chief Hayes knows about it now and he'll deal with it."

"You seem awfully confident in his ability to wrangle supernatural baddies," Sam noted as I sat on the edge of the bed and took a sip of tea.

I could feel its effects instantly. The tension in my shoulders ebbed away and I slumped toward the pillow. "He's not bad at his job, you know," I said, through a yawn. "Besides, he actually took me seriously when I told him about what I thought happened to Ronnie. Maybe we're finding a way to coexist finally."

Sam made a scoffing sound and as I fumbled to set the teacup back on the table, he vanished. I curled up beneath the blankets, ready to let Maggie's magical blend take effect and chase away the nightmares. After all, there was little chance an actual vampire would wind up crossing my path. I wasn't *that* unlucky, right?

7

Mercifully, I slept without dreaming the rest of the night. When I awoke the next morning, it almost felt as if nothing was amiss. But as I walked downstairs, tucking my High Time shirt in, I recalled my chat with Sam and his dislike of vampires. He'd said he didn't like that they could hurt people. But I wondered if he was jealous about the fact they could still interact with the living, and not just those with supernatural gifts.

"You look pensive," Tania said as I entered the kitchen.

"Just thinking about vampires," I answered, earning side eye. "Apparently ghosts don't like them much."

"You mean a particular ghost doesn't like them," she corrected.

"It's just interesting, that's all," I retorted.

"Learning is a good thing, but not if you obsess over it."

"I'm not obsessing." I accepted the plate of eggs and bacon she handed me and settled at the table. "Beau is worried about our safety. I'm just trying to protect us."

Tania made a dismissive noise. "Well, just make sure that protective streak doesn't interfere with your actual job."

"Don't worry, it won't." After a few bites of food, I asked, "What are you up to today?"

"Oh, nothing much. I need to run an errand to the butcher. I have a few recipes I want to try, but they need specialty cuts."

"I'm sure they're going to be delicious," I said.

She laughed. "Darcy, you don't need to butter me up. I'm not upset with you. I suppose sometimes I just feel like I'm the one who should be protecting you."

"Well, I appreciate it."

My phone alarm buzzed, letting me know I needed to be on my way to work. I hurriedly finished breakfast and set the dishes to soak. I was halfway to the front door when Tania called out after me.

"Oh, before you go, I have something I need to ask you."

I pivoted. "Yeah?"

"Would you mind if I took some of the aloe plants? Maggie had asked if I could bring her some for the infused lotions she was working on. I'm sure she meant to ask you, but you've both been so busy with work and your trip."

"Of course, she can have them."

"Great. See you later."

"Bye."

Despite the sun shining overhead, I couldn't help casting a glance over my shoulder on the short walk to High Time. I let out a long exhale once I was safely inside the grow room.

"Come on, Darcy, you're being ridiculous," I chided myself under my breath.

So, vampires were real. That didn't mean I was on their hit list or that they even knew I existed. Fretting about it wouldn't do me any good. Nor would it help the new crop flourish. Yet, I had trouble focusing even as I sat amongst the seedlings with their soft whispers of what they could be a running commentary in the back of my mind. I couldn't shake the thought that there was something using our town as its personal hunting ground. Surely tracking down a vampire wasn't stepping on Chief Hayes' toes. After all, I wouldn't be interfering with the police investigation into Ronnie's death. And Ginny had given me a good place to start.

But I'd wanted to do some digging into Devina Coombs. So, as I channeled some power into one of the smaller seedlings, urging it to grow and catch up with the others in the tray, I opened a browser on my phone and typed her name into the search bar. It only took me three tries to get her name spelled correctly thanks to one-handed typing.

My search yielded a website where Devina purported to be an expert on all things vampire. She claimed to be able to protect against them with 100% success. What I couldn't see was what made her such an expert. If she had such great knowledge and wanted to attract people to believe her, why not share that information? The lack of specificity made me question her legitimacy, but if Ginny believed her, then there had to be some kernel of truth buried deep down.

I resolved to visit Devina after my shift, just to sate my curiosity. Setting my phone aside, I focused on the flora around me, borrowing some of the hopeful energy from the plants. I wouldn't exactly call it a contact high, but maybe a magical one?

By the time my shift ended, I was feeling relaxed. I had a text from Maggie, letting me know she'd picked up another shift at the hospital and would call me when she was done. I wanted to tell her that I thought she was working too much and question whether this was a response to Ronnie's death. I knew she carried the weight of things like that more than most. I also knew firsthand that her biggest fear was her magic failing to save someone. But I didn't nag her.

Instead, I headed to the boardwalk to enjoy the summer air and browse the handful of stalls that usually popped up at this time of year. I passed vendors offering artisan handmade jewelry and Brookhaven t-shirts. I offered a wave as I walked, recognizing some of the sellers as High Time clients. A surprising number of business owners were regulars. I reached the end of the boardwalk, where Maggie and I had gotten on our boat over to Haven Island when I spotted a familiar face.

"Vinnie? Are you okay? You look terrible," I called.

He looked at me, the dark circles under his eyes prominent and stowed his phone in his pocket. "Hi,

Darcy. Just tired. I haven't been sleeping great the last few weeks."

I didn't have to ask why. Just seeing the investigation board in the police station suggested he'd been preoccupied. "Any luck figuring out what happened to Ronnie?"

He shook his head. "They're still running tests. His widow has been distraught though. And not much help."

"I feel so bad for Mindy; losing the person she loved so suddenly. Is she still in town?"

"Admitted to the hospital actually."

My heart skipped a beat, and my stomach did an uncomfortable flip. "Did something happen to her?'

"The doctors think it's just shock. She wouldn't leave his side for hours."

We barely knew each other and yet I felt drawn to the woman. Maybe even a semi-familiar face would help break through the grief making her ill enough to warrant a hospital stay.

"I hope you figure out what happened to Ronnie, and it brings closure to her."

"Me, too." He barely stifled a yawn.

"When's the last time you slept?" I probed. "I'm sure Chief Hayes would prefer his best deputy to be fully rested."

He gave me a small smile. "Thanks for that. Not feeling very good about the job right now."

"If you wanted, I could probably convince Sage to give me some edibles. Maybe even let me use the employee discount. That way you wouldn't have to buy them. Might help you sleep. Or some of Maggie's chamomile tea?"

"While I appreciate the offer, I'm okay. But I think I will try to get some rest."

"What were you doing down there?" I called.

"Huh? Oh, just checking in with the harbormaster to see if any other boats were out on the water over the weekend."

Does he think someone from town might have snuck over to the island to attack Ronnie?

"Makes sense."

"Too bad it was a dead end," he sighed, yawning again.

"Do you want me to walk you home?" I offered.

He waved his hand at me to dismiss my gesture of support. "I can manage. Thanks."

"Okay, see you around."

I watched him walk away and couldn't help following him at a distance, just to be sure he made it to his destination. Lucky for me, I'd decided to head to the hospital, and he lived only a few streets over. If nothing else, even if Mindy wasn't accepting visitors, I could wait for Maggie's shift to end.

Finding Mindy's room wasn't difficult, and a nurse confirmed that visiting hours were still in effect for another hour. I paused at the door, watching the young woman in the hospital bed. Even at this distance I could see her eyes were bloodshot and red-rimmed, and her skin was pale.

I knocked on the doorframe to announce my presence. She turned at the sound and I exhaled a breath I hadn't realized I'd been holding. For a moment, I'd feared her pallor was due to bite marks, but her neck was unblemished.

"Hey, Mindy, I don't know if you remember me. I'm Darcy. My girlfriend and I were with you when we brought Ronnie over from the island."

She nodded. "What are you doing here?"

"The deputy mentioned you'd been admitted, and I hoped a sort of friendly face might help cheer you up. I can't imagine being in the hospital in a strange town does much for healing."

"You probably think I'm crazy. Or having a breakdown."

"You just lost your husband unexpectedly. I'd be worried if you weren't a bit of a mess."

That earned a small half smile, and I crossed the

threshold and moved to sit at her bedside. "Is there anything I can get you? Or anyone I could call to come be with you?"

"My parents are going to fly in. They're in Tempe right now."

My knowledge of the United States geography was rubbish, so I just nodded. "That's good that they're coming. They can probably help you make arrangements for Ronnie."

"Sometimes I still don't believe it. But they showed me his body and he was so cold."

"I'm so sorry this happened."

Don't get involved.

The voice in the back of my head sounded distinctly like Tania's whispered the warning, but I couldn't help myself. "I know he was acting a bit odd when Maggie and I happened on him at the cove. But was he acting strangely before that?"

"I mean, I told him it was stupid to steal those flowers. He said he just wanted to shower me with beauty. I told him that was a sweet idea, but I didn't need him getting arrested."

"What about yesterday?"

"I slept in late. Too much wine. And when I woke up, he was gone. But it didn't seem like it had been that long."

"What makes you say that?"

"Well, his side of the bed was still warm."

"Had he taken anything with him, like his phone?"

Her brow furrowed. "I didn't notice. God, am I that unobservant I can't remember if my husband took his phone before he ended up dead?"

"You are not a bad wife. You didn't know you had any reason to be suspicious."

Mindy let out an audible sigh and wiped her eyes. "Looking back, he did seem a little out of it the night before. But I figured it was just the alcohol. He wasn't really much of a drinker, but he liked to pretend he could handle it when we were in groups."

"The police are going to figure out what happened," I told her. "And I hope you can get back on your feet once your parents get here."

"Thank you." She reached out for me, the cords of her pulse monitor tangling around her elbow.

I stood and bent over to allow her to hug me. "What's that for?"

"You didn't have to come see me. You don't even know me. But I really appreciate someone actually caring enough to see if I'm okay."

"I know what it feels like to be alone somewhere unfamiliar." I gestured to the hallway outside her room. "Plus, Maggie, my girlfriend, is finishing her shift and I figured I could surprise her."

"You two seem really great together," Mindy said. Color had returned to her cheeks, and she looked a little less haunted. Maybe a small kindness and company had been all she'd really needed. At the very least, it made me not as much concerned that her husband's attacker had gotten to her, too.

Her words about Maggie and I resonated in my ears. I smiled wide. "Yeah, we are." I offered another quick hug before leaving Mindy to rest.

I found my way to the elevator and took it down to the main floor, following the exit signs to get back to the Emergency Room entrance. I hated taking up space inside and had gotten a few disapproving looks from the charge nurse in the past, so I headed for the parking lot. I knew there was seating outside and the fresh air would do me good. Plus, I wouldn't have to wait too long for Maggie to wrap up her shift. I made it just beyond the automatic doors before I pulled Maggie's number up on my phone, sending a quick note in reply to her earlier text message.

> Hey, I know this kind of ruins the surprise, but I thought I'd stop by after your shift. I'm out in the parking lot when you're finished.

As I walked the distance from the edge of the automatic doors to the far end of the building, I spotted Tania's VW Bug in one of the stalls. Momentary confusion gave way once I remembered Tania had said she was giving the aloe plants to Maggie. But surely, she wouldn't do it at the hospital.

On my second pass along the wall, my phone rang with an incoming call from Maggie. "Hey, didn't think your shift was over y—"

The sound of a struggle over the line cut my words short. I froze, ears straining to pick up on what was happening. I could hear grunts, and something gave a decidedly body-like 'thump.'

"Get off!" Maggie's voice came through the line.

"Maggie, where are you?" My voice was high and squeaky.

She didn't respond. Panic sent my heart racing double time and I groped at the wall to keep upright. I wasn't the one being attacked—not this time—and yet I felt phantom pains on my body. My stomach sloshed like the time I'd been drugged. And my body tingled, little fires igniting along every nerve ending as if I were being poisoned.

More grunts and muffled sounds came through the phone's speaker before it started crackling. In some part of my brain, I knew I should try to patch in the police. They'd know what to do, but I couldn't make my fingers move.

The line went dead.

My fingers went numb, and my phone clattered onto the pavement. Where was Maggie? Was she injured? I'd done nothing but stand here like a helpless idiot. In the distance, I heard car tires squeal against pavement as someone drove off in a hurry. My vision was tunneling to black, and I didn't see who it was. Except in that moment, I didn't care who it was. I needed to find Maggie. *Now.*

8

I forced myself to take a deep breath, hold it for a count of ten and exhale. It was enough to beat back the tunneling darkness in my vision and I could finally feel my legs again. Maggie needed me. Swallowing the lump rising in my throat, I raced back through the automatic doors and skidded to a halt at the charge nurse's desk in the Emergency Room.

"You need to check in with the reception desk," the woman behind the desk said in a flat tone.

"Sorry, I'm looking for Maggie Henley. She's been shadowing some of the doctors on their rounds. She just called me, and it sounded like she was in trouble. I need to know where she is." The words tumbled out of my mouth so fast even I couldn't make sense of them.

Maybe this woman was used to people giving her information in a panicked rush, because she picked up the receiver from the phone cradle in front of her and a loud beep echoed in the space. "Maggie Henley, please report to the ED charge nurse station."

"That's not enough. She sounded like she was injured. The phone went dead. Please?" I begged, fighting back tears.

A stout woman in medical scrubs with a greying bob haircut hurried down one of the halls that led deeper into the hospital.

"You're looking for Maggie?" She locked gazes with me.

"Yes. I think she's in trouble."

"She was with me for rounds today, but she said she needed to take a few minutes to get something from a friend. She said they were meeting in the employee parking lot. Come on, I'll show you where it is."

I could have hugged the woman if it wouldn't have slowed down our trek through the hospital to the employee parking lot. It was the direct opposite side of the building from the lot where I'd seen Tania's car.

I couldn't say why, but the moment we stepped outside, dread washed over me. I scanned every car looking for Maggie. After the first two rows yielded nothing, my chest began to tighten as I recalled the sound of squealing tires.

"Maggie?" I called out, my voice hoarse from terror.

Finally, in the fourth row of cars, we found her. Her car was missing, but she was lying on the pavement, a nasty gash on her forehead. The aloe plants Tania must have brought were sitting on the ground beside her. The pots were shattered with soil strewn around my girlfriend. I fell to my knees and bent over her body, only allowing myself to relax when I heard her breathing and felt the rise and fall of her chest with my hand.

"I'm going to get a gurney," the doctor said.

That left me trying to rouse her. I did my best to probe around Maggie's head, checking for any other injuries. Thankfully, it appeared to just be the one on her forehead. I shook her shoulder lightly.

"Maggie, can you hear me?"

She gave a soft moan, and it took what felt like hours

for her eyes to flutter open. Her pupils were dilated and sluggish, but she was definitely awake. She started to turn her head, but I moved to be in her eyeline.

"Just lay still, they're getting a gurney for you." I reached for her hand, giving it a squeeze. "You're going to be okay."

"Tania," she managed to get out just as the doctor appeared with a nurse and the promised gurney.

"Easy now, let me check everything before we move you," the doctor told Maggie, getting down on the ground beside her. She did a quick check and looked over at the nurse. "I'm going to need a C-collar just until we get inside and do some scans."

The nurse hurried forward with the brace, and they secured it around Maggie's neck before easing her into a sitting position. When she didn't pass out or complain of pain, they maneuvered her onto the gurney and began to wheel her inside. I trailed them, unsure if they would let me join her. We were dating, but I wasn't family.

They raced through the halls and stopped at a door marked Restricted. The doctor turned to me. "You need to contact the police and get them down here. I don't' know what happened, but I can tell you Maggie didn't do this to herself."

I hated not being with her, but the doctor was right. I called 9-1-1 and waited for the dispatcher to come over the line.

"Emergency services," Chief Hayes' voice came over the line.

"Chief? You're answering nine-one-one calls now?" I asked.

"Miss Ingram, you better have a good reason for calling." I picked up on the exhaustion in his tone. Just like Vinnie, I bet he hadn't slept much lately.

"Maggie's been attacked at the hospital. I don't know exactly what happened, but she was unconscious when I found her in the parking lot."

"I'll be there in five minutes."

"I'll be in the Emergency Room waiting area," I told him and ended the call.

It only took me two wrong turns to make my way back to the Emergency Room. The charge nurse gave me a worried look as I passed, but I didn't share the news about Maggie's condition. I was more focused on connecting with Chief Hayes.

True to his word, he walked through the doors five minutes after I'd ended the call. I'd been pacing in front of an empty row of chairs and nearly rushed him when he appeared.

"Tell me what you do know," he said and gestured for me to sit.

My body thrummed with nervous energy, fueled mostly by the fact I didn't know what was happening with Maggie. I forced myself to sit anyway. "I came by to see Mindy. Vinnie told me she'd been hospitalized, and I just thought a friendly face might cheer her up. Then, I knew Maggie was working an extra shift shadowing today, so I was going to wait around for her."

"And where were you?"

I pointed to the visitor parking lot. "Just out there. I'd texted her that I was waiting and then a minute or two later she called me. I don't know if she meant to, but all I heard was grunting and the sounds of a struggle. At one point I heard her tell someone to 'get off,' but I have no idea who it was."

"Can you remember anything else about the call?"

"The phone went dead not long after. I remember hearing tires screeching somewhere, but I didn't see it. I was sort of panicking."

"Did you find Maggie?"

"Yes. She's with the doctors now."

"Show me where you found her."

Part of me didn't want to leave the Emergency

Room area in case they brought Maggie back down. But the chief needed to see where I'd found Maggie. So, I led him through the same corridors the doctor had taken me along to get to the staff parking lot. We moved past the four rows of cars to the spot where I assumed Maggie's car had been. Maybe whoever had attacked her stole it? The aloe plants had remained where they toppled onto the pavement.

"She was laying here with a nasty cut on her head. But she didn't seem to have any other injuries."

"You didn't notice any bite marks?'

"No. But honestly I was just trying to get her to wake up."

I should have checked, knowing what I did about the dangerous creature allegedly roaming our streets. For a brief moment, I understood Mindy's guilt for not noticing that something was off about Ronnie before his death.

"Thank you. I'll get someone to cordon this area off and we'll have the technicians come down to process it."

"Can I go back in? I need to know that she's okay."

In a much kinder, gentler tone than I could ever

recall hearing him use, Chief Hayes said, "Yeah, of course. Come on."

I let him take the lead on the way back in this time and thankfully we didn't take any wrong turns. We arrived in the Emergency Room, and I spotted the grey-haired doctor who'd brought Maggie inside. Certainly, she wouldn't have left Maggie alone. Sure enough, when I approached the curtained bay, Maggie was lying in a bed. She sported a bandage on her forehead and the neck brace had been removed.

I was at her bedside in an instant. "How are you feeling?"

"A little hazy if I'm honest," she said, her words came out slow. Her pupils had returned to normal size and tracked the movement around her more easily. She spotted Chief Hayes. "Rick?"

"Darcy called. Looks like you were attacked."

Her hand moved to the wound on her head. "Yeah, I ..." she looked around again. "Where's Tania?"

A sinking feeling gripped my stomach, and I held the bedrail tighter in an effort to ward off nausea. "She wasn't with you."

"Why don't we start with what you can remember?" Rick suggested, still using that gentle tone.

"I went to put something in my car," she began.

"The plants?" I suggested. "Tania said she was bringing you some aloe."

"Yes. She'd brought them and I was putting them in the car. I'd also borrowed a sweater of hers, so I told her I'd return it at the same time. And then, something hit me."

I really didn't like where this was going. "You called me."

"I did?"

She made a move as if to pick up her phone, but it wasn't there. I hadn't seen it on the ground near her earlier, but I hadn't been focused on that in the moment.

"I heard a struggle and you told someone to 'Get off,'" I replied. "Are you sure you don't remember who hit you?"

She shook her head and winced, pressing her hand to the side of her head. "It's kind of fuzzy still. But I think they took my car."

"Had you finished exchanging items with Tania before this?" Chief Hayes interrupted.

"I don't think so."

"I saw Tania's car in the visitor lot when all of this happened," I said, suddenly feeling the need to check and make sure that my friend's car was no longer at the hospital. Although, if Maggie had been assaulted, Tania wasn't the type to leave her alone.

"It was still there when I arrived," Rick said, his brow furrowing with concern.

"Wait, are you telling me someone attacked Maggie and what ... abducted Tania?" I said, disbelief coloring my voice.

"Unless we can find her, I would say that is most likely what happened."

"No one would want to abduct Tania. Everyone in town loves her," I protested.

"Yet it appears that might be the case," the chief responded. "Maggie, did the person who hit you say anything that you can recall?"

"I don't know ... maybe? It's still so fuzzy."

"Head trauma can cause difficulty forming and retaining memories. Let's give Maggie a chance to rest and see if she remembers anything else," the doctor said, cutting the questioning off.

That seed of guilt had taken root in me thinking I could have done something more for Maggie grew as I realized that I'd stood frozen while another of my friends was taken.

"Darcy, you're going to need to come to the station and give another statement about this," Chief Hayes said.

"Yes, of course. But can I go back to the B&B first? Just to make sure Tania didn't walk home. Maybe she saw me and thought I might need the car?" It was a ridiculous excuse, but he accepted it.

"Just as soon as you can."

I stood, but Maggie grabbed my wrist. "I'm sorry I couldn't stop them."

"You don't have anything to be sorry for. I promise, I'll be back just as soon as I can." I leaned in and kissed her. As I pulled away, I cast a surreptitious glance at her neck. To my relief no bloody wounds marred her skin.

I left the hospital behind and stopped at the VW Bug. The keys were missing, and I spotted empty grocery bags in the front seat. Tania must have made this her first stop before she headed to the butcher for the specialty meats she'd been after.

I hurried back to Main Street and took the last half block to the B&B at a flat-out sprint. The front door slammed against the wall as I entered the foyer.

"Tania? You home?" I called as loudly as possible.

No answer.

I checked the kitchen and dining room, both of which were empty. From there I took the stairs to the second floor two at a time, but her bedroom was vacant, too.

"Sam?" I tried.

Relief flooded me as his incorporeal form materialized at the top of the stairs. "Why are you shouting?"

"Tania's missing. I think she might have been abducted. I—I hoped ... I hoped she was just home and had left her car at the hospital."

Somehow, Sam's already translucent complexion paled. "No one would hurt her. Everyone loves Tania."

"I know. But Sam, someone attacked Maggie. Stole her car and Tania's missing."

"What are the police doing about it?"

"They're looking for her. I don't know if there's any security cameras or anything at the hospital, but I'm sure they'll check that, too." I spun in a circle. "I just wish there was something I could do to help."

Wait, there is something I can do.

"You've got that look in your eye, Darcy. What are you planning?"

"Tania was giving Maggie some aloe plants when this all happened. They're still at the scene."

I doubted that Chief Hayes had gotten the crime scene techs down to the hospital yet. Still, I likely had a very narrow window to get there and see what the plants could tell me before it became off limits. And I'd prefer not to get caught trespassing.

My heart hammered in my chest as I ran along the far perimeter of the hospital. As I went, I kept an eye out for cameras, anything that might give me a hint that the police had non-magical means to catch the person who'd abducted Tania. There weren't any on the side I passed, but I thought I spied one over the entrance leading into the hospital from the staff parking lot.

The chances it had enough range to catch what happened here were slim, but I sent up a little prayer that it would be enough to give Chief Hayes something to work with. And if I found anything of note from my snooping, I would tell him. With Tania missing, there was zero reason to keep things to myself. I might be getting better at controlling my magic, but there was no chance I could do this on my own.

The parking space and the ruined plants remained unobstructed. I scanned the ground for Maggie's missing phone, but nothing stood out. I bent and scooped up the nearest aloe plant that still had its roots deep in the soil.

"Okay, let's see what you can show me."

9

Seeing through plants had been something I'd first found I could do during my last stint of solving mysteries on Haven Island. It felt almost as natural as breathing these days. I could tap into the plant's sentience and see whatever had occurred when it was around. I dug my hands into the lump of soil until I found where the base of the plant connected to the roots.

Deep within me, I felt my magic surge forward, ready to pull me into the plant's reality. Power crackled along my skin, sending the tiny hairs on the backs of my arms on end as it funneled into the point where flesh met leaves.

I opened my eyes to find myself in the VW Bug, parked outside Beekman Family Butchery. Tania stood at the door, bag slung over her shoulder. She disappeared inside.

So, she had gone to the butcher first.

She reappeared moments later empty-handed. She climbed behind the wheel, setting the bag on the floor and put the car in reverse. Sometime later—plants don't actually have a sense of time—Tania pulled into the visitor lot at the hospital. She picked up her phone and dialed a number.

"Hola, Maggie, I hope this isn't a bad time to drop off the plants for you?" she said.

There was a pause as Maggie responded.

"Okay, I'll come around the back."

She stowed her phone in the center console of the car and picked up both potted plants from the passenger seat. She carried them around the side of the hospital. She approached Maggie's car, but Maggie wasn't there.

Time jumped again and Maggie appeared, something slung over her arm as she approached. Tinted by the plant's point of view, it looked muddy, but as she set it on the hood of the car, I recognized it as one of Tania's red cardigans. Not something either of them needed for the summer weather. Maybe it had been a winter-time loan that Maggie had just remembered?

There was still nothing to suggest the imminent

attack. Maybe this plant hadn't been aware enough to see what came next?

Maggie unlocked the car and opened the back seat door. "Thanks again for bringing these."

"Of course, and thank you for returning this," Tania answered, gesturing with one of the pots toward the cardigan.

Something large cast a shadow over both women and before either knew what was happening, Maggie was shoved up against the car, the door slamming under her weight. Her phone fell out of her pocket, landing on the ground. Somehow it had called me without her meaning to.

Their attacker grabbed Tania, pressing something over her mouth. She went limp within moments and fell to the ground, the pots landing on the pavement and shattering as I'd found them.

Maggie wasn't done fighting. She shouted, "Get off!" just as I'd heard her and lunged for the hulking form now hovering over Tania's limp frame. With another shove, the assailant knocked Maggie's head into the ground and pressed the same cloth to her mouth.

Whatever was used to drug the both of them could have been the reason Maggie's memory was hazy. Somehow, the attacker had kept their face hidden. Even still, I could tell they were heavy set and strong, easily hoisting

Tania over their shoulder and tossing her in the back seat of Maggie's car. They moved to climb behind the wheel, stepping on Maggie's phone as they went. They seemed to realize it was underfoot, and picked it up, tossing it into the passenger seat. After taking a few moments to hotwire the vehicle, they peeled out of the lot, leaving Maggie behind, unconscious.

It hadn't been nearly as helpful as I'd hoped. But I'd confirmed how they were attacked, and that Tania had indeed been taken. Only the vague details I'd been able to uncover felt useless to the police. Still, I'd promised myself I would report anything I saw to Chief Hayes.

I set the clump of soil and plant back on the ground and dusted off my hands. I heard voices approaching and hurried to put distance between myself and the scene. Unfortunately, I wasn't fast enough to escape Chief Hayes's eagle eye.

"Darcy, come with me."

"I didn't do anything," I protested, even as I realized I had dirt smears on my pant legs.

"Process what you can," he told the techs accompanying him before he turned his full attention to me.

He ushered me a few car lengths away from the scene. My heart hammered in my chest as the chief looked at me. I expected a harsh response, but once again, his tone came out gentle.

"I know you're worried about Tania, but interfering in an active crime scene isn't the way to help her."

"I know I shouldn't have, but I saw what happened," I replied in a whisper.

His brow furrowed. "You told me you were on the other side of the building when this happened."

I gestured to the spilled soil and discarded aloe plants. "I was. But remember I have this connection with plants, and the aloe showed me what happened leading up to Tania's abduction."

"Alright, walk me through it."

I wasn't thrilled to be recounting what I'd witnessed with the crime scene techs within earshot. It was one thing telling the Chief of Police about my magic, but the techs were strangers. "I watched Tania meet up with Maggie. Someone came up from behind threw Maggie into the car and drugged Tania. Then they hit Maggie and tried to drug her too."

"Did you get a look at their face?"

I shook my head. "Maybe because the plants aren't exactly sentient like you or me it didn't recognize the face. But the attacker hotwired Maggie's car. And they took Maggie's phone."

"Did you see anything else?"

I closed my eyes, trying to run through what I'd seen through the plant's awareness. "She stopped at the butcher shop before she came. It didn't look like she was there for long, and she didn't leave with anything." I let out a frustrated sigh. "I don't know if that's helpful or relevant, but that's all I saw."

"It allows us to track her movements. It helps," Chief Hayes responded. "You should go back to the B&B."

"I should check on Maggie first," I protested.

"She needs her rest. Go home."

I realized there was something he wasn't saying, but I couldn't put my finger on what. "Do you think this is connected to the other cases?" I blurted.

The gentleness faded from his demeanor. "What other cases?"

"Chief, I'm not blind. I saw the board in the station when I told you I thought there might be a vampire involved in what happened to Ronnie."

Chief Hayes let out a prolonged exhale. "For now, all we know is Tania's been taken. There's nothing to suggest this is connected to anything else that's happened recently. Now Darcy, *go home*."

I wouldn't put it past him to try and send Vinnie after me to make sure I complied. I hated feeling so helpless. Tania could be anywhere by now. Why couldn't the aloe plant have caught a glimpse of the abductor's face?

"You can come into the station tomorrow to give your statement," he added, as if reading my mind.

That settled it. I detested having to go home, but was out of reasons not to be there. Besides, this was a case where I couldn't afford to antagonize law enforcement. I left the hospital parking lot behind, deciding there was one last detour I could make, if I was lucky. Fortunately, Tania's car still sat in the visitor lot. I opened the passenger door, looking around the interior for anything that might jump out at me.

I'd hoped maybe I was wrong, and Tania had in fact gotten something from the butcher. I searched for a receipt, hoping it had simply fallen between the seats. Nothing. I felt hot tears prick the backs of my eyes as I eased the door shut and sunk down to the barrier in front of the car.

Part of me knew it wasn't true, but I couldn't help feeling like my magic had failed me. And for the first time in nearly a year I resented the magic flowing through my veins. What good was it if I couldn't use it to help find my friend?

My vision blurred the longer I kept the tears at bay. Letting them out appeared to be the only solution. They streamed down my cheeks, bringing with them the frustration and anger that I hadn't been able to stop Tania's abduction. My fury had built up with those overwhelming emotions, especially now with Maggie lying in a hospital bed.

Get up and do something about it.

The voice in my head sounded an awful lot like Maggie's this time. Somehow, it was enough to snap me out of my downward spiral and I stood up. Just because I hadn't been able to prevent my friends from getting hurt, didn't mean I couldn't find a way to help them. If the last year had proven anything, it was that when I got stuck in a mystery, I didn't let go until it unraveled.

Besides, maybe some sleep would help me think and piece things together I couldn't see right now. So, I walked back to the B&B, watching people pass by on the street. I wondered if they knew one of the pillars of the community had been taken. In my mind, there should have been more panic, more of a frenzy to start looking for her. But I had to remind myself that her abduction was only a few hours old at most. There was barely enough time for the police to complete their initial canvas of the area.

I didn't expect to be accosted upon walking through the front door, but I nearly walked through Sam as I stepped into the hall. The bottom of the banister rippled as Beau dropped his camouflage.

"What do you know?" Sam demanded; his usual flamboyance muted by his clear worry over Tania's absence.

"Tania was taken. I don't know by whom, and I don't know where they've gone. But the police are looking."

"She was taking plants. Did you see what they saw?" he continued, hovering an inch off the ground, floating back and forth in a ghostly imitation of pacing.

"That's how I know what happened. They stole Maggie's car, too. And they took her phone. I honestly have no idea why she's been taken. Has there been any calls?"

"What, like a ransom?" he scoffed.

I threw my hands up and walked around his incorporeal form. "I don't know! My friends don't typically get abducted. I'm kind of at a loss right now."

'Hunted. Taken.'

Beau sounded morose in my head. I couldn't help but scoop him up and hold him close to my chest. "I don't want to believe that this has anything to do with Ronnie or vampires. But in a way, it would at least give me something to go on."

"So, what do we do now?" Sam's anger ebbed.

"I'm going to try and get some sleep. I'll check on Maggie in the morning. Hopefully by then, Chief Hayes will have some leads. Besides, I've got to go down and give my formal statement anyway."

"How can anyone sleep at a time like this?" Sam muttered and disappeared.

I didn't tell him I intended to use a heavy dose of product Sage had given me as a holiday present at Christmas. It was the only way I would get any rest.

I WOKE THE NEXT MORNING FEELING FAR MORE invigorated than I'd anticipated. Sage's edibles were far more potent than I'd realized. Still, I needed all the energy I could get if I was going to be of any use to Tania or Maggie. I had no doubt Sage would give me the day off once she knew what had happened, but I was likely to only get the one day. I needed to make the most of it.

"Hey, Sam," I called as I hastily poured coffee into a travel mug and took a bite out of a piece of toast.

The ghost materialized on the other side of the kitchen. I didn't think ghosts slept, but he looked more rested and less sullen than yesterday. I took that as a good sign. "You rang?"

"Can you poke around town today, see if anyone's talking about what happened? Maybe someone else saw something?"

"Anything to bring Tania home," he said and after offering a brief bow, blipped out of existence.

I sensed Beau behind me, and I pivoted to see him lounging on the counter next to the stove. "I know you want to help, too, mate. I need to go see how Maggie's doing, but I promise, if I need you, I'll come get you."

'Keep you out of sight.'

"I know you can. But I also know that using your magic on me wears you out. My gut tells me we're both going to need all our strength to bring her home safe."

I left the chameleon behind as I hurried at a brisk pace to High Time. Thankfully, Sage was in early, and I caught her before most of the rest of the kitchen crew arrived.

"I hate to do this, but I'm going to need to take today off," I said, catching Sage's attention.

"You don't look or sound sick. What's going on?" she replied.

I swallowed the lump in my throat. "Tania's been abducted and Maggie's in the hospital. I have to give Chief Hayes my formal statement and, I don't know, maybe try to find something that they can go on."

Sage set down the clipboard she'd been holding and wrapped me in a tight embrace. "Do what you have to do."

Luckily, by the time I made it to the hospital, visiting hours were in effect and a nurse led me up to a room where Maggie lay against the stark white blankets. Her red hair stood out and mercifully, her pallor had normalized. Her eyes opened when I shut the door behind me, and she pushed herself into a sitting position.

"Hey, how are you feeling?" I said, settling on the end of the bed.

"Like an idiot. I should have done more."

"You tried to stop some lunatic from taking Tania. You're lucky all you got was a head wound. It could have been so much worse." I reached up and took her hand in mine. "I could have lost you."

"Does Rick have any leads?"

I shook my head. "None that he's sharing with me. I did use my magic on the plants she'd brought for you. I saw what happened. At least from the plant's perspective anyway."

"It's still kind of hazy," Maggie said.

"The assailant used some sort of drug to sedate you both. Maybe it interfered with your short-term memory?"

"Maybe." She rubbed at the side of her head, just below the edge of the bandage. "It's going to sound weird, but there is one thing I remember."

"Yeah? What's that?"

"The scent of roses and something like blood."

Roses? Blood? My mouth went dry as a thought hit me. There was only one place we'd encountered anything remotely close to roses in the last few days. As much as I hated to admit it, I had a sneaking suspicion I was about to be on my way back to Haven Island.

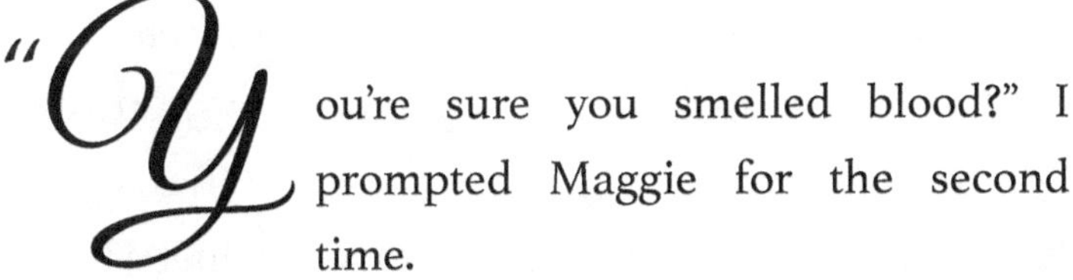

ou're sure you smelled blood?" I prompted Maggie for the second time.

"Yes." She squeezed her eyes shut, as if trying to recall the sense memory. "I don't know how to explain it, but I smelled blood. Like old blood or something."

"And the roses?"

"It's just too hazy, Darcy. I'm sorry."

I wanted to push her, but I knew it wouldn't get us anywhere. If Maggie's memory was intact, it would come back to her in time. Although, I couldn't help but note bitterly that Maggie's magic was generally the one we'd rely on for bringing something like this to the surface.

"You don't have to apologize," I finally said and leaned in to kiss her on the cheek. "All you need to do is rest up. I'm going to see Chief Hayes and figure out if they've gotten any leads."

"Promise me you won't go snooping alone," Maggie said, catching my wrist in her right hand.

I made a mental note she didn't tell me to not snoop at all. "I won't. You have my word."

"We're going to get her back," Maggie added as I reached the door.

"I know we are." There was no other option.

I left the hospital and stopped just beyond the automatic doors, staring at the visitor lot. Tania's car had vanished, likely towed. I did owe Chief Hayes my statement, but there was one thing I needed to follow up on first.

Plants clearly don't perceive time the same way people do. So, what I'd seen from the plant's point-of-view could have been skewed. And for all I knew Tania had only gone on in to order the specialty meats she'd mentioned. It could explain why she didn't walk out with anything in hand. It was time to pay the butcher a visit.

Despite the promise I'd just made to Maggie, I strode down Main Street unaccompanied. Beekman Family Butchery came into view at the end of the street farthest from the waterfront, nestled three storefronts down from Ginny's. I'd never paid it much mind. Tania handled the food and the few times I'd picked up anything, it had been at the local grocery on the west side of town. White lines painted on the pavement designated the two parking spaces allotted to the butcher shop. I could almost picture Tania's car idling in one of them. I repressed a shiver as I pulled open the door and stepped inside. A tiny bell above the door chimed upon my entry.

Much like many of the shops in town, the space on the customer side of the counter was limited. I could see an area obscured through plastic sheeting that led into the back of the shop. The telltale whir of freezers running filled the small space with a constant buzzing. I looked up at the handwritten chalkboards hanging above the counter, displaying the shop's cuts of the day. I noted that the date hadn't been changed in a couple of days, and none of the specialty meats I'd expect to hold a place of prominence were listed.

I closed my eyes and inhaled, taking in the smell of the place. I could pick up on the obvious hints of raw meat from being packaged and weighed on the scale at the far end of the counter. But there was something else in the air, something floral, almost like ... *roses*. It couldn't have been a coincidence.

"Hello? Mr. Beekman?" I called.

Clattering from the back caught my attention and I braced myself against the counter as a thick-set man pushed the plastic barrier aside. He stepped up to the counter, laying a cloth on the surface beside him. Mr. Beekman sported a dark brown apron over his navy button-down shirt. The sleeves were rolled up past his elbows and I could see the marks from where gloves had pinched his wrists from being the wrong size.

"We're not really open yet, Miss," he said.

"Oh, I'm not looking to buy anything, I was just hoping you could answer a question for me."

He arched a bushy brow at me and let out a sigh. "Yeah, all right. Make it quick, though. I've got things to do."

"Of course." I drummed my fingers on the counter. "You know Tania Alvarez, right?"

He let out a snort. "Everyone knows Tia Tania in this town."

"Well, I'm one of her boarders. I work at High Time. Anyway, she mentioned yesterday that she'd be coming down to order some specialty meats."

I waited for him to fill in any details that would

confirm he'd seen Tania yesterday. Beekman stared at me, his gaze penetrating. "They're not in yet. Should be here by the end of the week. Which is what I told her when she came in yesterday."

Confirmation he'd seen her.

"Oh, I see. I offered to pick them up for her when they're ready, but she didn't tell me what she'd ordered. Do you maybe have a record of it? I want to be sure I get everything when they're in."

He let out a sigh of annoyance, but reached beneath the counter and pulled out a ledger. "She ordered six lamb shanks, four cuts of filet mignon, and some ox tail."

I had no sense of how much that might have cost or just how specialty they were, but it did seem more exotic than a small town butcher would offer. "I don't see any of that listed up there." I gestured to the sign overhead.

"Hadn't gotten around to adding it. Look, like I said, it will be in Friday."

"Sure. Thanks, I'll come by then," I said.

I turned to leave and spotted a vase of vibrant red roses nestled on a shelf above the cash register. "Lovely flowers," I noted.

He glanced at the arrangement and let out a cough. "From my mother. She hates the smell of raw meat. Thinks this might turn less people away."

Interesting.

"Thanks again, and sorry I bothered you so early. I'll be back to pick up that order at the end of the week."

He waved me off, picked up his cloth, and retreated to the back of the shop. As I left the storefront behind, I couldn't shake the feeling something was off about Beekman. I didn't know anything about the man, but I just got bad vibes from him.

As I turned left, my feet carried me almost by sense memory toward Ginny's, I heard a car pull up to the curb beside me. Vinnie rolled down the window and leaned out. "Hi, Darcy. Chief Hayes wanted me to make sure you come in to give your statement."

"I was heading there now," I replied.

He gestured to the passenger side of his squad car. "Climb in, I'll drive you."

I was about to protest that I was perfectly capable of walking to the station, but the stoic look on his face suggested it was better not to argue. So, I rounded the hood of the car and settled in the passenger seat.

"Has there been any word?" I asked as we pulled into the back of the station.

"Afraid not," he answered and led me through the back entrance into the station.

I followed him past the interview room, the evidence lock-up, and the station's sole cell to his desk. Chief Hayes was nowhere to be seen. Vinnie settled at his computer, and I took the seat next to the desk. I caught sight of the board sitting just outside the chief's office. I hadn't gotten a good look at it the last time I'd been here, but something looked different.

"Luckily, this shouldn't take too long," Vinnie, said, drawing my focus back to him. He tapped away at the keyboard for a moment, before turning the monitor towards me. "Chief Hayes put together a preliminary statement last night. If you could just take a look and make sure it's accurate, then I'll print it and you can sign it."

I read over what Chief Hayes had written, noting that it was very accurate. It was far more than I would have expected from him, what with the stress of what looked to be a series of murders and now a missing person's case. "This looks right."

"Darcy, could I ask you something?" Vinnie sounded nervous.

"Yeah, of course. I can't promise to have an answer, but you can ask."

"You didn't notice anything strange around the B&B in the days leading up to the abduction, did you?"

"If I'm honest, I was away with Maggie all week-end. And everything seemed fine around the place. I didn't get a sense that Tania had issues with anyone that would prompt them to take her like this, if that's what you're thinking."

"You're sure, you didn't notice anyone hanging around who shouldn't have been there?"

"No, nothing like that. And besides, everyone likes Tania."

"I know. I just can't wrap my head around who would want to attack her. Because, between you and me, this felt planned."

I leaned in. "I got the sense from talking to Maggie that she was drugged with something."

Vinnie worried his lower lip. "I probably shouldn't be telling you this, but the hospital did find chloroform in her system."

"That would explain Maggie's hazy memory when I talked to her this morning." I wasn't ready to point fingers at anyone in particular, so I kept the clue about roses and blood to myself.

"Okay, well if everything looks good in your statement, I'll print it out."

"Thanks."

He fiddled with the mouse for a minute. "I keep forgetting that the printer out here needs new ink. Give me a minute. I'll have to use the one in the chief's office."

"I've got nowhere to be," I replied. When he gave me a confused look, I added, "Sage gave me the day off on account of everything that's going on. I'll head back to the hospital after lunch to see how Maggie's doing. I don't like the thought of her being alone there."

Vinnie gave a curt nod and disappeared into the chief's office; the door swinging shut behind him. I eased myself out of the chair, wincing as the cushion groaned from removing my weight. I paused mid-motion, but when Vinnie didn't reappear, I darted around his desk to look at the board.

Pictures of four individuals—three men and one woman—were laid out in neat columns. Their names didn't register in my mind. Even in a small town like Brookhaven, I didn't know everyone's names. Each had a date of death listed, ranging from two weeks ago to six weeks. They all had puncture marks on their necks and were missing organs; lots of them. All but the woman had been found without their livers and kidneys. She'd been missing a spleen in addition to her lungs. Given the missing body parts, I would have expected the crime scene photos to be gorier, but there was a distinct lack of blood on them. Like someone had drained them dry.

Bile rose in my throat at the thought of the horrors these people had been through. I could only hope they'd already been dead when their bodies were violated in such a manner. Realizing I wouldn't have another reason to be here without sneaking in, I pulled out my phone and snapped a photo of the board for later examination.

The sound of paper feeding through the printer in the chief's office signaled my snooping was done. I retreated to the chair just as Vinnie appeared. He handed over the printed pages and a pen, and I scribbled my signature with the date at the bottom.

"Is there anything else I need to do? Or can do?"

"Not right now."

"What happened to Tania's car? It was at the hospital lot yesterday when I left. But when I went by this morning to see Maggie, it was gone."

"We impounded it for evidence. We don't expect to find much there, but we had to look anyway. We'll take good care of it."

At least my hunch about its location had been confirmed. I didn't expect them to find much either. My quick search didn't turn up anything either. Without a word, Vinnie took my signed statement and put it into the file with Tania's name sitting on his desk.

I was about to leave and head back to the B&B to formulate my next move when the phone on Vinnie's desk blared, making us both jump in surprise. He recovered first, scooping up the receiver and pressing it to his ear.

"Brookhaven Police," he said. "Oh, hi chief."

There was a long pause as the chief relayed whatever message he had over the line. Vinnie's cheeks paled the longer the silence went on. Finally, he made a strangled coughing sound. "Understood. I'll … I'll be right there."

"Vinnie, what's the matter?" I prompted, placing a hand on his upper arm. He swayed under my touch.

"We got a report. Someone spotted a car down by the docks. It's Maggie's … Darcy, they found Maggie's car."

"What about Tania?"

He shook his head. "I don't know. But I have to go."

"I'm coming with you," I said, marching toward the back of the station in the direction of his car.

"You can't come," he said weakly.

"Please, Vinnie. I need to know what's happened to Tania. And I can help. I promise I won't touch anything, but maybe I'll notice something."

"Fine, but you don't do anything unless I or the chief says it's okay."

"You have my word."

With that, we retreated to his car and even though it wasn't strictly necessary, he flipped on the siren and slammed on the gas to get us to our destination faster. As we zoomed through the back alleys of town, my heart hammered painfully in my chest. I wasn't a police officer or a private investigator or anything of the sort. However, a few months ago, Ginny Hayes had told me I was something of an amateur sleuth and at the time I'd leaned into that moniker, because my family had been in danger. Well, it was time to don that identity once again. Tania was just as much family as Piper to me. I was going to do everything I could to find her, even if the possibility of what awaited us at the docks terrified me.

Please let Tania be all right.

11

espite Vinnie's gas-pedal-to-the-floor driving, it felt as if it took us forever to get to the docks. When the edge of the waterfront finally came into view, my breath caught in my chest with a strange sense of relief. Maggie's car looked undamaged. In the short time between when Vinnie received the chief's call and our arrival, I'd conjured up the image of a burnt-out husk of metal. Obviously, I'd been watching too many crime dramas.

Able to breathe easier now, I followed Vinnie to where the vehicle sat cordoned off with police tape. No crime scene technicians were present yet. So, Chief Hayes must have established the perimeter himself. Speaking of the chief, he stood off to one side with a young man I didn't recognize, his notepad in hand.

Chief Hayes caught sight of me and dismissed the young man. Vinnie must have realized we'd been spotted, because he hurried forward to intercept Rick.

"She insisted on coming," he blurted.

"I'm not surprised she did," the chief answered, not taking his eyes off me. "Vinnie, why don't you finish taking that young man's statement? He's the one who spotted the car and called it in."

"Yes sir." Vinnie's mouth hung open, as if he wanted to say more. After a beat, he thought better of it and hurried off to do as instructed.

"Have you had any more of your, uh ... plant visions that might give us a hint of what we should be looking for in the car?" Chief Hayes asked in a quiet tone.

I hadn't seen anything new, but maybe there was something I'd missed in the vision before? I'd been so focused on seeing what happened to Tania and Maggie, I hadn't paid much attention to the rest of the scene. I closed my eyes and focused on the memory. It played across my eyelids like a film— vivid and detailed. I watched again as a figure drugged Tania and Maggie and stole away with my landlady.

At first nothing else stood out to me. But, as I made it play over again, I saw something. As the assailant hotwired the car, whatever he used to subdue my friends had slipped between the seats. "Miss Ingram, did you hear my question?" Chief Hayes said, jolting me out of the memory.

"Yes, sorry. I did see something. The assailant dropped something between the seats." After a moment, I added, "I already told Vinnie I wouldn't touch anything or interfere." I hoped my words would preempt the same lecture a second time.

To my surprise, the chief held out a pair of latex gloves. "Not without proper protective measures you aren't."

I let the moment of surprise pass before I took the proffered gloves and tugged them on. I gave an involuntary cringe as the powder within them started to dry out my hands.

"You said you saw the assailant drag Tania into the car before driving away?"

I ducked under the police tape and followed him to the car. None of the doors showed signs of being touched and it felt wrong, even with the gloves on, to be the first to open it. So, I gestured to the back driver's side door. "Yes, in there."

Chief Hayes opened the door and bent down to fit his torso into the car. "There might be some hairs in here to confirm whether she'd been in it." He took half a step back and straightened. "You're sure she hadn't been in Maggie's car recently?"

"I'm sure."

I didn't see any obvious signs of blood, which had to be a good sign, and buoyed my hope that Tania was alive. As I studied the backseat, a thought hit me.

"They took Maggie's phone. It should still be here. They tossed it up front." Without waiting for permission, I darted around the front of the vehicle and pulled open the passenger door.

But there was no phone.

Had they taken it with them?

I crouched and began to feel around on the floor and wheel well to no avail. Nothing hard or phone-shaped appeared. Refocusing on what I'd seen dropped, I searched between the console and the side of the seat. My fingers did brush against something soft and I tugged it free.

The rag.

Gingerly, I held it up to my face and took a

shallow breath. I noticed something chemical about it, but I could also pick up the hint of something like old blood and ... roses. Just like Maggie had said.

"Chief, I found something," I called.

I set it upon the passenger seat as he appeared over my right shoulder. "It was wedged down there." I pointed to where I'd discovered it. "Maggie said she'd been drugged."

"We'll make sure we get it tested."

I wasn't sure about sharing my theory on Mr. Beekman, since I had no motive for why he'd attack Tania or Maggie.

However, as I moved out of the way so the chief could get a picture of the cloth, I spotted a little monogramed B.B. in the corner and the script matched the butcher's logo.

"I know they put Maggie's phone in the car before they left. They must still have it with them," I told the chief just as the crime scene techs pulled up.

"We'll look into it. You have my word."

In all the time I'd lived in Brookhaven, I'd never seen the station have the necessary equipment to track phone locations. Not that I spent a lot of time there, but I just got the sense they were stuck a few decades behind the times when it came to that sort of thing.

Luckily, I knew someone who was a whiz with computers. I still remembered Maggie hacking into a phone nearly a year ago like it was nothing. My girlfriend had many talents. But I'd have to wait until she was back on her feet before I broached the topic. And it wouldn't really be illegal, seeing as it was her phone.

I moved away from the car and back to the civilian side of the police tape so the techs could begin their work. Chief Hayes followed me, and I peeled the gloves off, shaking my hands as I did. I didn't know how they could wear them for long.

I looked at our surroundings. This far down on the boardwalk and pier didn't get much foot traffic, even in the summer. It seemed a strange place to leave the car. "Do we know how long the car was here?"

"Just because I let you look at the car, doesn't mean I'm able to share details of an ongoing investigation with you," Chief Hayes replied.

"It's just, we're right on the water and that means Tania could be anywhere."

"I understand how worried you are. Tania is my friend, too," he answered. "I swear we are doing everything we can to bring her home safely."

"I just feel like I should be doing more."

"The best thing you can do right now is be there to support Maggie during her recovery."

"I can do that."

I left Maggie's car and the police behind, making my way down the boardwalk back into the populated areas. There were more pedestrians around than I would have expected for late morning. There were a mix of locals I recognized and tourists milling about. I spotted the shack that served as the harbormaster's station and remembered that Vinnie had been looking into what boats had been leaving the area recently in his investigation of Ronnie's death and the other deaths over the last six weeks.

I wouldn't have a reason to ask him outright, but if I brought a peace offering, the harbormaster might be more willing to chat with me. And luckily for me, he had a standing order at High Time.

AFTER MAKING A QUICK TRIP BACK TO HIGH TIME— Sage had given me a confused look when I placed an order for the harbormaster's usual, but filled it anyway—I approached the shack. I knocked on the wooden frame and a man with a shock of greying hair that stuck out in two tufts on either side of his head appeared.

"Hi there," I said and held up the bag of edibles. "I work over at High Time, and I know you've got a standing order. Sage asked me to bring it by."

He gave me a suspicious look for all of three seconds before he accepted the bag and opened it, inspecting the contents. "Sage doesn't usually do delivery, but I'll take it."

"Might be something new she's considering," I lied.

"Well, I appreciate the service."

"You're the harbormaster, right?" I said as casually as I could manage, leaning on the door to keep his attention on me.

"That's right."

"So, you know all about the boats that come in and out of here?"

"Sounds like you already know what I do. Something specific I can help you with?"

"Actually, there might be. I've only lived in Brookhaven a short time and I've only ever seen boats coming and going from around here. But the boardwalk extends pretty far. Is this the only place boats can launch from?"

"Well, generally speaking this is for commercial

vessels. Fishing boats, passenger boats, and the like. They all dock down here. The far end—" he gestured the way I'd come, "that's for private craft."

Private, like for people who owned mansions on the island and needed a place to dock on this side of the water. "I didn't realize we had many people in town who owned their own boats."

"Most folks on this side of the water don't. It's the rich ones over on Haven Island that dock their boats here. Not that they come this way often."

"Sorry if this is a silly question. I don't know much about boats. But if you own a boat, do you have to register it, like a car?"

"Course you do."

Brilliant.

I still didn't have a solid reason as to why Mr. Beekman would go after Tania, but it couldn't be a coincidence one of his butcher cloths had ended up in Maggie's car smelling of roses and chemicals. If he was the one behind Tania's abduction, and he'd left the car at the far end of the pier, then perhaps he'd done it because he had a boat waiting there. Though it still didn't tell me where he could have taken her. It couldn't have been far if he was around this morning to answer my questions.

"Thanks again for answering my questions. And enjoy your edibles."

The harbormaster's eyes widened a little in surprise at the abrupt end to our conversation, but he gave me a little wave and ducked back into his shack. I needed to see what I could find out about Mr. Beekman and why he might have gone after Tania. And I was going to need all the help I could get.

I checked the time. It wasn't nearly as late I'd expected and certainly too early for lunch. But not too early for a second morning cup of coffee. I powerwalked up Main Street and right into Ginny's. She was seated in her usual spot and pivoted upon my entrance, giving me an expectant look.

"You seem like you were expecting me," I said tentatively as I sat beside her.

"Rick may have given me a heads up that you'd paid a visit to a certain scene, and he wanted me to make sure you weren't running off doing anything daring."

"I was just chatting with the harbormaster about boats."

"Why the sudden interest in boats? I thought you disliked open water."

I could feel her pulling the words out of me.

"They found Maggie's car near where the private boats dock. I think maybe whoever took her used a boat to get her out of town."

"I knew you were smart," she said as someone set a cup of coffee in front of me.

I was about to protest that I hadn't ordered anything, but realized it would be rude to decline what could end up being a free cup of coffee. "Can I ask you something?"

"You can ask, doesn't mean I'll know the answer. I know a lot of things, but I am not omniscient."

"What can you tell me about Beekman Family Butchery?"

"Oh. They've been in business for years. Brian Beekman runs the place now. But his uncle ran it before him. His dad was never much for the family trade."

"Is Brian's mum still alive?"

"No. She died when he was a teenager. Why?"

"I saw him this morning and he's got some roses in the shop. He said his mum told him it made the place smell less unpleasant."

"She could have, but it wasn't any time recently."

"And has he done things like bring in expensive specialty cuts of meat before? It's just I know Tania stopped by the other day to place an order and it seemed like something out of the ordinary. It wasn't even up on his sign yet."

"Not that I can recall. The family has always been pretty simple. I mean, sometimes they'll get things in that are kosher, but that's been the extent of how fancy they get. Why the sudden interest in him and his business?"

"Because Maggie smelled something like old blood and roses when she and Tania were attacked. Also, I found a rag like the one Mr. Beekman uses in Maggie's car." I took a sip of coffee. "And then there's the roses I saw in his shop. Something just isn't adding up."

"Why would Brian want to hurt Tania or Maggie? He's known them for years. They're probably two of the last people I'd expect to garner grudges in this town. They're just too upstanding and decent."

"I haven't a clue why he would target them. He doesn't happen to own a boat, does he?"

"Not that he ever mentioned to me. But I think his uncle did at one point. But he died about three years back. That's when Brian took over running the business."

If that uncle had died without anyone else to inherit that boat, it could have gone to Brian and his father. It still didn't answer the question of what would prompt him to take Tania, though.

"None of this makes any sense," I sighed, hanging my head.

"Well, detective work isn't easy," Ginny pointed out.

No, it wasn't. But I'd gotten some of what I'd hoped out of Ginny—confirmation that the Beekman's had access to a boat. I could check and see what I could dig up at the library on ownership. Maybe that could point me to a motive.

Vampires.

The supernatural creatures popped into my head without warning. There was still the matter of those victims with the puncture marks in their necks and the missing organs. Had Tania inadvertently happened upon something she wasn't meant to? Could that be what led to the attack and her abduction?

"Thanks for the help. And the coffee," I told Ginny as I downed the rest of the liquid in the mug.

"And if Rick asks me where you're headed, what should I tell him?"

"I'm off to the library," I said truthfully. After that, I would finally make the trip out to see Devina. And as I'd promised Maggie, I wouldn't go alone.

Sam may dislike vampires on some weird ghostly principle, but I knew for a fact he wouldn't let me go see someone who might have intimate knowledge of them without him. And Maggie didn't say my accomplice needed to be alive.

12

The library was nearly empty when I arrived. That didn't surprise me. Most people were either at work or out and about elsewhere. As I walked into the room with the public computers, I spotted a familiar face tucked into one of the overstuffed armchairs with a newspaper spread in his lap.

"Morning, Gerry," I greeted.

"Oh, morning Darcy. Don't usually see you here, especially on a workday," he replied.

The fact he didn't look at me with pity suggested news of Tania's abduction hadn't made the rounds. I let out a slow exhale. "Tania's been taken. I'm trying to see what I can find that might help the police locate her."

Gerry set his newspaper aside and stood. "What do you mean taken?"

"Someone attacked her and Maggie yesterday afternoon. They took her, and made off with Maggie's car, too."

"Shouldn't everyone be mobilizing, trying to look for her?"

"I'm not in charge. You should talk to Chief Hayes. But it doesn't look like he thinks she's still in town."

I didn't need to pull him into my theory about Brian Beekman. Gerry was a nice bloke. I felt bad for him since he'd lost his son on his son's wedding day. Andrew's daughter—one he didn't know existed—had murdered him to keep him from marrying her friend. And for ruining the lives of his other ex-wives. Gerry had been coping as well as could be expected. But he didn't need to get tangled up in this mystery.

"I'm honestly only here for a few minutes, just to look up some things. And then I need to check on Maggie in the hospital."

"Right. I'm going to go down to the police station and see what I can do to help." He reached out and pulled me into an awkward side hug. "Thank you for letting me know what's going on."

I nodded mutely and waited for him to release his grip on me. In short order, he hurried off, his paper abandoned on the chair, and I stood in the room alone. I settled at one of the computer terminals and navigated to Brookhaven's town website. Finding the registration page for vehicles was simple enough and mercifully there was a section listed specifically for boats and other watercraft.

"Let's see if you had the means to get Tania out of town, Brian," I muttered under my breath and typed in his name.

A single result populated on the screen, providing a convenient link to the history of a small motorboat. I glanced over the boat's specifications including model and size. I assumed most modern boats could fit at least two people in them and possibly even more, but not comfortably. The title details were listed in chronological order, listing a Martin Beekman as the boat's original owner, purchased nearly two decades ago. The record then jumped to three years ago, at which time the title was transferred to a Bruce Beekman, where it had remained to present.

"Definitely not Brian, then."

It was logical to assume Bruce was Brian's father, but it didn't hurt to check. I navigated back to the town's website and looked around for birth records. Thankfully, it wasn't going to charge me just for searching someone's name. After all, it wasn't like I was requesting a copy of the man's birth certificate. But putting in Brian Beekman turned up one result.

"Born tenth November to a Susan O'Neal (Beekman) and Bruce Beekman," I read aloud.

So, his dad owned the boat now. That didn't mean Brian couldn't have access to it. I knew very little about Brian or his father. Ginny had said Brian took over the shop from his uncle when he passed away. She hadn't said a word about what Bruce did for a living.

Just as I was about to exit out of the browser, my phone rang with an incoming call. It was an unknown number.

"Hello?" I answered hesitantly.

"Hey, Darcy, it's Maggie," my girlfriend said on the other end of the line.

"Is everything all right?"

"Yeah, they say the chloroform has cleared my system and since the cut on my head was superficial and they're satisfied I don't have a concussion. So, they're releasing me."

"That's good news."

"It's going to sound silly, but do you think I could stay with you tonight?"

I smiled. "I was going to insist you do. I don't want you to be alone right now."

"I know Tania usually doesn't lock the front door, but I didn't want to just go there without telling you."

"I'll come by and walk you back. Besides, there some things you need to know about the case."

"See you soon."

"Bye."

I closed out of the browser and logged off the computer before heading back to the hospital. I had to wait in the lobby area for Maggie to be released. As I sat there, I overheard two nurses on their way out. Both were dressed in scrubs I associated with the Emergency Room.

"You know, I haven't seen him for a few shifts," one of the nurses remarked.

"That's rare for him. He's always on nights."

"I heard someone say they thought his dad was sick, so he'd gone out to look after him."

"Then that's probably where he is."

I couldn't help wondering who the 'he' was they were discussing. I didn't have time to ponder it long, because the elevator doors opened. Maggie walked out, dressed in a pair of oversized sweats. I raced to her side.

"I'm really okay. I promise," Maggie said and waved me off. "I just want to get my own clothes and settle in somewhere familiar."

"I can do that."

TWENTY MINUTES LATER, WE SAT ACROSS FROM EACH other in the B&B's kitchen. Maggie nursed a cup of chamomile tea. Sam hovered over her right shoulder and Beau perched on the table at her right elbow.

"I appreciate you worrying about me guys," she said, glancing first to the chameleon and then over at Sam.

"You're one of our favorite people," Sam said, no hint of sass in his tone.

"So, what exactly did you find out?" Maggie directed her question to me.

"Rick found your car abandoned at the far end of the boardwalk. And they found the cloth that was used to knock you and Tania out. I know that whoever took Tania grabbed your phone. But it wasn't in the car. At least not when I looked."

"You went crime scene crashing in broad daylight?" Sam scoffed.

"It was sanctioned by both Rick and Vinnie," I retorted before continuing. "The cloth had the logo of Beekman's Family Butchery on it. And when I talked to Brian Beekman this morning, he seemed kind of off."

Maggie's brow furrowed in thought. "It could have been animal blood. Like what's created from handling raw meats."

"He had fresh roses in his shop, which was strange, too. And his father owns a boat. Or well, his uncle did, but then he died and now his dad owns it."

Maggie held up a hand to stop me. "You think Brian Beekman took Tania? What for?"

"I don't know. But something tells me it's got to be connected to what happened to Ronnie and all those other people who turned up dead."

"Other people?" Maggie's features clouded with confusion.

I retrieved my phone from my pocket and opened up the photo I'd taken of the board at the police station. I passed it to her. "For the last six weeks, they've found all these people dead, missing loads of vital organs. They had puncture marks in their necks too. Just like Ronnie."

Maggie set her tea aside and studied the image. She pressed two fingers to the screen, zooming in on the information. The confusion that had clouded her features a moment ago disappeared, replaced by disgust. She remained silent as she studied the rest of the information.

"What? What do you see?" I prompted.

She passed the phone back to me, and I enlarged the image, trying to see what had caught her attention, but nothing immediately stood out.

"The organs they're missing," Maggie began. "Are ones you might find on an organ transplant list. The same ones that people who have a lower chance of getting through legitimate means might seek out elsewhere."

"You mean like the black market?" I said, failing to hide my own disgust.

"Exactly. And then there's the fact they're all the same blood type."

I manipulated the image to show the bottom of the board where someone had added the words 'Blood Type: B+' under the first victim. Moving the image horizontally revealed the same text under each of them.

"That is odd," I agreed. When I looked up from the screen, I saw Maggie's cheeks had paled. "What's wrong?"

"Tania is B-. I know because she's donated blood at the clinic a few times."

"So, maybe they didn't know?"

She shook her head. "We were both there and Darcy ... I'm B+. What if whoever took Tania was actually after me and just got us mixed up?"

I didn't want to think that my girlfriend had been the target of this whole scenario. "But why would they want you?"

"They're clearly going after people with a certain blood type."

"Okay, say that's true. Any idea how Brian Beekman would know that information?" I zoomed out of the image to show the photos of the victims. "None of these people look familiar."

Maggie reached for the phone again. "They look vaguely familiar. Like I've seen them before. But I can't remember where."

"Could they have come through your clinic?" I suggested.

"It's possible. I'd need to check my records."

"Okay. Why don't you do that while Sam and I go run an errand?"

"What sort of errand?" Sam interjected, flitting to hover beside me.

"Well, I've been meaning to see Devina Coombs, but with Tania being taken, I got sidetracked. And I think finding out what she knows about vampires might point us in the right direction." I glanced at Maggie. "And I made a promise not to go off snooping solo."

"You do know how I feel about vampires, right?" Sam said.

"I do. But I'd feel safer having someone who can't die there with me."

"Fine."

"You said they didn't find my phone," Maggie said as I stood.

"Not that I saw."

"Have you tried calling it to see if it's even still on?"

Of course! "No, but if I do, could you track its location?"

"It should be linked to my computer, so yes. If it's still on."

I was hesitant to part from my phone. I didn't know what meeting Devina would entail and I didn't like the idea of being out of communication with Maggie. She appeared to sense my apprehension, because she said, "I'll try it from the clinic phone."

"As soon as we're done at Devina's, I'll come to the clinic," I promised, and Sam floated ahead of me toward the front door.

'Will protect her.'

Beau blinked up at me from the kitchen table. His tail curled gently around Maggie's wrist. "Thank you, mate. I know you'll look after her."

Maggie scooped the reptile up and positioned him on her shoulder where he nestled against her neck and disappeared from view. I leaned in and gave Maggie a kiss on the lips. "If I haven't told you lately, you're bloody amazing."

"Go talk to your vampire whisperer and let's bring Tania home."

Sam hovered on the porch as I pulled the front door shut behind me. "You're uncharacteristically quiet," I commented as I pulled up Devina's website on my phone to double check the address.

"I'm allowed to be worried about my friend," he answered as we started toward the edge of town.

"Of course. Just, you seem more subdued than I'd expect. We're going to get Tania back," I said.

"You don't know that. You can't know that!" he argued. "She could have kicked me out when she took over running the place. But she let me stay. She gave me a home."

"You've still got one," I reminded him.

"Do I?" His attire shifted to all black as we walked. "If she dies and there's no one left to give me sanctuary, do I just disappear forever?"

I didn't have any answers for him. Until that moment, I hadn't known Tania had to give him permission to stay. I just assumed Sam had died in the vicinity of the B&B and was bound to the place. "I wish I knew what to say, but the rules of being a ghost are new to me. And once this is all over, you and I are going to have a proper chat about how it all works."

"I still don't see how you can be so positive about finding her. Those other people all turned up dead."

"I have to believe we'll get her back, because if I let myself spiral into the what ifs, I don't think I'll be able to pull myself out again," I admitted. "Right after it happened, I could feel my magic starting to retreat, like the fear of losing her triggered something in me that shut down and regressed the progress I've made."

"So, you hang on to the hope, because otherwise you lose who she helped you become."

"Yeah, I guess so. Tania is strong. I have to believe

that she's a fighter, too. She's out there and we're going to get her back."

"We're going to get her back," Sam repeated, and his jacket lapel took on a hint of sequin sparkle.

We passed by Tyson's Treasures, and I noted that the front door sported a 'Closed' sign. That was unusual. I filed it away as a curiosity for another time and continued on just past it to a squat single-story house with blackout curtains in the windows.

"So, what exactly do we know about this woman?" Sam asked as I approached the front door.

"Just that she claims to know a lot about vampires." I was still unclear how she had such intimate knowledge. And hadn't Ginny said she wasn't a vampire?

"I'm only going to say it once, there are no good vampires," Sam said as the door swung open before I could even raise a hand to knock.

"Come in. I've been expecting you," a deep, alto voice called from within the house.

I exchanged an apprehensive glance with Sam before taking a step forward. If he could have, I suspected Sam would have taken my hand as a sign of solidarity. Instead, he hovered as close as I'd ever seen him without passing through me.

I crossed the threshold and felt a strange shift in

the air around me. I got the distinct sense that there was nothing alive in this place except for me. *Please don't let this be the last thing I do.* The entryway fed into a single room off to the right before heading straight back into what I assumed to be a kitchen and perhaps a bedroom. I turned at the first opening to find the room dimly lit. I could just make out a figure by a reading lamp in the corner.

"Devina?" I asked, my voice suddenly hoarse.

"As I said, I've been expecting you," the figure replied as she leaned into the light to reveal pale skin and wide icy blue eyes.

Time to have an interview with a vampire.

13

*P*art of me wanted to go deeper into the room, but the part that operated from a place of fear stayed put. Maybe it was the lack of lighting or the fact she'd somehow known I was coming that set my nerves on edge.

"You're the one who wanted to come," Sam prompted in my ear.

Some help he was.

Swallowing my fear, I took a tentative step into the room and approached what I assumed was a sofa. Devina leaned out of the dim lamp light, and I heard the sound of fabric rustling and the lamp grew brighter. As my eyes adjusted, I realized she'd had a scarf hung over the lamp to dampen the brightness.

"How did you know I was coming?" I asked once I was settled in the chair.

"I don't get out much, but I hear things. Ginny Hayes likes to think she is in control of the rumors in this town, but she's not the only one who can coax a secret out of people."

"Oh."

"And she came by this morning to tell me what happened to Tania and that you'd been asking questions."

I heaved a small sigh of relief that she wasn't clairvoyant. "I think Tania was taken by a vampire. But up until a couple of days ago, I didn't even know they were real."

"Most people don't truly believe in their existence," Devina noted.

I couldn't help but notice the way she said 'their' and not 'our.' Everything about the scene suggested she was a vampire. She appeared not to like sunlight or have any need for heating or cooling systems.

"I can see you want to ask me something. Might as well get it out now," Devina commented with a knowing smirk.

"You're ... not a vampire?" Before I could stop myself, the words poured out. "It's just that your website said you had a lot of intimate knowledge about them, and I suppose I assumed that's because you were one … but didn't want to admit it to people. If you are, I'm sure there are people out there who would be prejudiced against you just because of who or what you are." I glanced at Sam.

Devina gave a toothy grin, and I noted the lack of sharpened canines. "One needs an air of mystery in this business. People mostly contact me online about my expertise and it helps business when they think I could be a vampire."

"But you're not," I repeated.

"Not for lack of trying I'm afraid. Sometimes, these things just don't stick."

"How does that work?" The words were out of my mouth before I thought better of them.

"To explain how it failed, I suppose I ought to explain how one would succeed first," Devina answered and rose from her chair, moving through the open space between my chair and hers.

"Here we go," Sam muttered.

"You're not here for colorful commentary," I reminded him before I realized I hadn't confirmed whether Devina could even see Sam.

"I understand your feelings against the undead," Devina said, staring Sam straight in the face. "For a time, I despised them, too."

"You were probably jealous," Sam scoffed.

"In a way, yes. But I can sense that you, too, are jealous of them in your own way. Getting to touch, to feel, to see those they love, and be seen."

"No offense, but Sam and I have already had this conversation. I respect that he dislikes vampires. Right now, I need to know what you know about them, because I think one of them has taken my friend. I'd like to get her back with a pulse still, thanks," I interrupted.

Sam's incorporeal form dimmed beside me, and I heard Devina exhale. I suppose breathing was a giveaway she wasn't undead. If she no longer had a heartbeat, then she likely had no reason to keep breathing.

"So, how does it work, becoming a vampire?"

"It works best when the person being turned is near death. The one who turns you must give you some of their blood after drinking from you." Her hand brushed the side of her neck. "If you're lucky you're so near death that the pain of it doesn't bother you."

I got the sense that wasn't her experience, and my heart ached a little for her pain. "So, they drink your blood, and you drink theirs. Then what? Do they have to bury you or something?"

"Nothing so elaborate. They just have to wait for your heart to stop. And then, if you're one of the lucky ones, you'll wake with prolonged life and a need to consume blood for the rest of your days." The forlorn look in her eyes sent a wave of sadness crashing down on me.

"Is it magic that extends their lives?" My voice came out in a whisper.

"Of a sort." Devina swept forward and threw herself down into her seat by the lamp again. "Perhaps that's why it failed to take with me."

"How do you mean?"

"Before I was this," she said and waved her hand from her head to her knees. "I was a witch, like you. Well, I suppose more like Ginny or Tania. My skills laid more in sensing what was to come."

"My nan's magic is like that," I offered. "So, maybe you can't be both?"

"I've questioned for years why it didn't take and I do believe it was because there was already supernatural essence in my veins."

"Forgive me if this is impolite. But if you aren't a vampire, why all the darkness and brooding?"

"Because I may not be undead and I may not crave blood, but I got left with the adverse effects of sunlight. I won't turn to ash or anything, in fact no vampire would unless you light them on fire, but it burns my skin. I find that my eyes are far more accustomed to the darkness these days, too."

"Is there any way you can tell if someone is a vampire just by meeting them?"

"These days it's harder; what with things like makeup that can make someone have a rosier complexion. And so long as they don't go out often in sunlight or get near a heart monitors, the only other thing that might give it away is that they're cold to the touch."

"What about mirrors?" I pressed.

Devina shrugged. "Guess that was a myth because they've still got reflections."

I closed my eyes, trying to conjure the memory of meeting Brian Beekman this morning. I hadn't had an occasion to touch him, but he hadn't looked particularly pale. Or maybe bad lighting had covered it up? And what about the marks on his wrists? I'd assumed that he'd worn gloves that were too small for him. Could a lack of a heartbeat somehow change how his body reacted to those sorts of things? And being around raw meat would certainly disguise the consumption of blood.

Could he be the vampire the police were after?

Pieces of it fit the narrative I was building in my

mind. The rag and the scents certainly lent credence to the possibility that he'd been the one to attack Maggie and Tania. I still didn't have a motive, though. Unless he'd been intending to take Maggie like she had thought. Not because she shared the same blood type with the other victims, but because she'd seen Ronnie and been involved in trying to save his life.

"Do most vampires drink human blood?"

"If they do, it gives them more of a passable complexion, but I've known some who relied on animal blood. There's even a movement online to push for it, because it's more human and leads to fewer untended new vampires," Devina replied.

Mr. Beekman gets another tick in the 'possible vampire' column.

"Anything else I should know about them? Super speed? Able to turn invisible? Hypnotize people?"

"They definitely can't turn invisible and no they can't transform into bats or fly. Speed, though, is something they do have."

I didn't have all the puzzle pieces sorted yet, but Brian Beekman was looking guiltier than he had before my arrival. "You're sure they can't mind control people?"

"Just because I haven't heard of it doesn't mean it isn't possible. Why do you ask?"

"Maggie and I were out on Haven Island over the weekend and one of the people staying at the mansion with us died. He had puncture marks in his neck. And not long before he died, he showed up out of nowhere, very dazed and confused. Almost like he'd been drugged?"

"It's possible. But most vampires who feed on humans don't tend to let them just walk away."

I opened my mouth to retort that poor Ronnie hadn't in fact gotten away in the end, but kept my mouth shut.

"I understand you want to help your friend. That's admirable of you, but vampires for all of their allure, can be very dangerous."

"Believe me, I wouldn't be looking for one if it weren't absolutely necessary. And if I could just point Chief Hayes in the right direction, I'd be more than happy to keep out of the way when the arrest goes down," I professed.

"I've heard about you, though. You don't let them take the lead. Not when you're invested, have skin in the game."

I took it for the dig it was. She wasn't wrong. But I would do what I could to ensure that Chief Hayes or Vinnie was there when I confronted Brian. No ransom demand or anything of the sort had been made, but my gut told me that the longer we went without rescuing Tania, the worse the outcome would be.

"One last thing before I go," I said, my body poised to stand.

"Yes?"

"Can I ask how long ago you tried to become a vampire?"

"About three years." She gave me a wistful look that slipped into something akin to despair. "You would have thought I'd see it coming. Oh, well. Nothing I can do about it now."

"Thank you for taking the time to speak with me," I said and offered my hand for her to shake.

"I hope it gave you the clarity you were looking for."

"I think it did," I replied and stood, showing myself out.

I waited until Sam, and I were back in the afternoon sunlight before I reached for my phone. I felt Sam's gaze on me before I could get past the lock screen.

"If you've got something to say, just say it," I said, not looking at the ghost.

"You have a theory on who you think took Tania ... and you're about to go off and confront them, just like she said."

"No, I'm not. I'm going to call Vinnie, tell him I have a suspect for him to investigate," I answered.

"And then you're going to confront them," Sam repeated.

"Not exactly."

"Darcy, what are you going to do?"

I needed to be sure that Brian was at the shop before I told Vinnie where to find him. And it couldn't hurt to see what he might be hiding in his back room. "I promise, I'm not going to confront him."

"If you get turned into a vampire, I'm never speaking to you again," Sam said and disappeared.

I hurried back toward the center of town. Ideally, I should have swung by the B&B to get Beau and see if he could conceal me while I snuck into the shop, but I didn't. The detour could be the difference between finding Tania dead and finding her unharmed. And I still needed to find a way back to Haven Island because all of the evidence seemed to be leading back that direction.

I made it to Main Street in record time, but I took a turn before I hit the row of shops that included

Beekman's Family Butchery. I slipped into the alley behind the storefronts and used Ginny's rear entrance—the smell of used coffee grounds was pungent enough to be a landmark— to guide me to the back of the butcher shop. There was enough space for a refrigerated truck to pull through and up to the back door.

I reached for the metal handle before stopping long enough to wrap my hand in the hem of my shirt to avoid leaving prints. The door opened into an industrial kitchen with several large freestanding freezers lining the back wall. The hum and buzz of the cooling units working overtime was amplified in the small space. I shivered at the drastic drop in temperature as I looked around.

There were a few animal carcasses, some marked up for being portioned out. Others just sat on slabs, waiting their turn to be butchered. Even in their current state, I was at a loss for what some of them could be. Maybe Brian had actually gotten in those specialty meats and was working on preparing them for orders.

The freezer farthest from the back door appeared to be the loudest, as if it was working harder than the other units. I approached it, casting a look around, half expecting Brian to appear. I appeared to be alone in the room. A quick check of the freezers offered up what looked to be normal freezer temperatures for storing meat. The one making the most noise, however, was significantly higher, reading at 35 degrees Fahrenheit.

I lifted the lid and bent down to study the contents only to stumble backwards when I realized I was staring at a pair of human lungs, packed with large bags of ice. There was something darker that could have been a liver or kidney, too. My mind flashed to the list of missing organs from the board in the police station.

A whole host of new questions sprang to mind. Was he eating them? Did vampires even need to eat anymore? Was he selling them and if so, to whom? Maggie had mentioned the organs were frequently sought after for illegal transplant. But that couldn't be right. Could it? Would a vampire really have a need for that sort of thing? Had this been what could have prompted Tania's abduction? And if that was the case, had Maggie really just been an innocent bystander caught in the crossfire or was she still in danger?

Biting back bile in my throat, I slammed the freezer lid shut and backed away. I unlocked my phone and dialed Vinnie's number, waiting while it rang. After the fourth ring, it went to voicemail.

"Vinnie, it's Darcy. I think I might know who is behind your string of dead bodies. I'm at Beekman—"

Pain erupted at the base of my skull. My hand went numb, and the phone clattered to the floor before my body lost the ability to stay upright. Seconds later everything went black and quiet.

14

A sense of movement slowly brought me back to the world. Movement and a bone-deep chill. My head throbbed and when I tried to reach up to assess the damage, I found my hands were secured together. I groaned and tried to free my hands, but they were stuck fast. Needing to better assess the situation, I forced myself to open one eye. Dark walls surrounded me on all sides—muted metallic grey with no windows. Opening the other eye allowed me to register that I was in the back of a truck; one traveling at speed. I turned my head just enough to see a freezer unit and my brain made the link. I was in a refrigerated truck. My joints were stiff from the cold, and it took me a few tries to even get my elbows to bend. When the blood finally began circulating again, I managed to lift my arms up to see that someone had wrapped duct tape around them. Trying to kick my legs revealed the same treatment around my ankles. The fact I could breathe easily sent a wave of relief through me that at least my abductor hadn't taped over my mouth or nose.

That did beg the question of how long I'd been unconscious. When Maggie and Tania had been attacked, their assailant had used chloroform. I didn't taste anything akin to chemicals on my lips and I wasn't disoriented in the same way Maggie had been. Could Brian be working with an accomplice? Or had my abduction been too spur of the moment?

The truck slowed and then stopped abruptly, sending me rolling towards the front of the truck. My legs slammed against the freezer unit, sending lances of cold and pain up my shin. I gritted my teeth to keep from crying out and revealing to my captor that I was awake. I closed my eyes until I could just make out the barest glimpse of the wall opposite me. I hoped it would be enough to convince Brian—or whoever had taken me—that I was still unconscious and unaware of my surroundings.

I heard the groan of a car door opening and shutting from the front of the truck. Rushed footsteps crunched on the ground outside and then the door to the back of the truck whined as they undid the outer lock and tugged the door open. I was grateful to have my eyes mostly shut, because the afternoon light was blinding after the muted grey of the truck's interior. The floor of the trailer shifted as more weight was added to it. I tensed as a blurry figure approached and hefted me into their arms. I could make out the scent of dried animal blood as my captor moved me out of the truck and into the summer air.

Definitely Brian.

I could just make out something dark looming ahead of us, growing larger as Brian walked. The darkness shifted as he turned, shouldering his way inside. The moment the door swung inward, and he stepped through, the overwhelming scent of roses assaulted my nose. It was enough to coat the back of my tongue, so it was all I tasted when I swallowed. Brian stopped walking after a few more steps and he lowered me to the ground, letting me flop over on my side.

An odd sense of excitement rippled through me. Brian didn't know I was a witch, and he definitely didn't know my powers stemmed from plants. He'd unwittingly given me an advantage in this scenario.

Still keeping up the guise of unconsciousness, I watched him through the slits in my eyelids. He paced back and forth before speaking.

"I need you to come take care of this," he said.

I opened my eyes just a touch wider to see a phone pressed to his ear.

"No, don't tell me you can't do anything. You owe me ..." After a pause, he added, "She's not going anywhere. You know where to find her."

There was another pause as the speaker on the other end of the line responded.

"I don't care what you do with her. I doubt anyone's going to miss her."

I picked up on the audible beep as the call ended. I wasn't about to let this man hurt me. But it was intriguing to know he was working with someone else. It sent my mind spinning with a whole host of new questions. Why would a vampire need an accomplice? Had Brian been the one who'd tried and failed to turn Devina? How much did this accomplice actually know about Brian's true nature?

Time to force Brian's hand and get him to admit what he knew.

I let out a low moan, catching his attention. I made a show of stretching and tugging at my wrists and ankles, feigning shock at their restrained state. I opened my eyes all the way to find Brian towering over me, framed on either side by elegant rosebushes, dotted with red and pink blooms. I could feel them trying to catch my attention, like little whispers in my ear, but too many to catch a single one completely.

"You should have kept your nose out of things," he said, his voice deepening in what I assumed was a menacing manner.

"I was just trying to find my friend," I answered.

His brow wrinkled for a moment. "And you thought she'd be in my shop?"

"I know what you're hiding," I retorted.

"Oh, do you?"

"You're the one who killed all those people Chief Hayes is looking into. The ones with the missing organs. That's why you took Tania. She found out what you were doing, and you had to keep her quiet."

"You think you've got it all figured out," he scoffed. "You don't know anything."

I pushed myself into a seated position, hands still bound together resting in my lap. "I saw the lungs in your freezer, Brian. I'm guessing you're selling them. Is that how you could afford to bring in the pricier stock for your shop?"

"A man's got to support his family."

"By selling human body parts on the black market? You do know you were going to get caught eventually?"

"Could I have been a little more careful where I left them when I was through, sure? But there was absolutely nothing connecting me to a single one of them."

I opened my mouth to counter his statement, but I couldn't. Aside from sharing a blood type—which wasn't information Brian would likely be privy to—they didn't appear to have any connection to the butcher.

"If you'd just stayed out of things, none of this would be happening now," Brian said, his tone softening. Almost like he was sorry he was going to try and kill me.

"You can turn yourself in. Come clean about what you've done. It isn't too late to make things right and let those people's families know what happened."

"I'm not going to prison," he spat.

Could they even keep a vampire in prison? Pushing the logistics of incarcerating an immortal being out of my head, I focused on my surroundings.

Every moment I sat here was more time his accomplice had to arrive. *His accomplice ...*

"You aren't the one killing them," I said as the realization dawned on me. "You were just taking what was left behind, weren't you?"

"Still think you've figured it all out, huh?"

"If you're protecting whoever you're working with, they aren't worth it. You don't really think they'd do the same for you."

He let out a bark of laughter. "You watch too many TV shows. You're not going to get in my head that easily."

He wasn't going to give me Tania's location and I doubted his accomplice would be any more forthcoming. He shifted his weight, eyeing his phone and I remembered I'd been in the middle of talking to Vinnie when Brian had attacked me in the butcher shop. With any luck, Vinnie had found I was missing and was looking for me now.

I couldn't wait for a rescue. Besides, I had all the tools I needed to make my own getaway sitting around me. I just needed to listen. I closed my eyes and reached inward for my magic. It shot to the surface and warmed me like the sun beating down on an unfurled leaf ready to soak up energy. I needed to free my hands and feet first, and then I'd have full control of the space around me.

Let's get rid of this tape.

The rosebushes nearest me fell to the floor with a loud smash as clay pots shattered. Roots and thorny branches tangled themselves around me, slowly wearing away the adhesive of the tape against my wrists. They wound themselves into the small gap between my hands and ankles. The plants dug into the tape from beneath, shifting back and forth in a sawing motion until the bonds finally snapped. Despite their sharpness, the thorns never once broke my skin or drew blood.

"What the ..." Brian trailed off as I opened my eyes again.

The bonds around my ankles and wrists fell away in tiny shreds, littering the dirt beneath me. Without realizing it, the roots and brambles had eased me to my feet, and started to twine around me in a defensive posture.

"Oh, I suppose I should have mentioned, you brought me to the worst possible place," I said, confidence bubbling up in my chest. "See, I'm a hedge witch and this place is literally made for someone like me."

Brian staggered backward, knocking more plants

to the ground as he went. I reached out a hand, and one of the branches nearest the door erupted, transforming into a slithering vine. It trailed after him as he vanished from my line of sight. I heard something clang and then a jolt of pain arced up my outstretched hand.

It took a moment for me to understand what had happened until Brian emerged holding a machete. I expected to see dried rust-colored stains on it, but the blade was pristine. As if it had never been used before. Seeing the weapon made my mouth go dry and cold sweat prickled under my arms and at the small of my back.

That confidence—cockiness really—faded as he brandished the weapon at me. In the distance I could swear I heard tires crunching over gravel. My heart leapt into my throat at the possibility that I was about to come face to face with Brian's accomplice. For a brief moment, that possibility paralyzed me. Somehow, I shook free of that fear as Brian took another step closer, waving the machete through the air in wide arcs.

Use what you've got to your advantage.

It sounded eerily like Tania's voice in my head, reminding me that I had far more at my disposal in this place than he did. I hated the thought of sacrificing these beautiful flowers to his blade. My head erupted with soft whispers from the flowers all around me.

Let us be your shield.

They were willing to take a hit for me. I offered up a silent thanks as I began making weaving motions with my hands. Much like I'd done in the B&B's backyard months ago, I wound the leaves and branches of the nearby bushes into a latticework of strength. I had just enough space to see Brian take a wild jab at the brambles. He swung again and again. Each time, I felt little jolts dance up my arms or skate across my collarbone as bits of the flowers I'd fueled with my magic fell to the ground, severed from their whole.

"You aren't going to get through," I called to the man as he continued trying to hack away at my barrier.

"How dare you use his flowers like this," Brian shouted.

"Brian, please, you don't have to do this. And you should know, the police are coming." That last bit was my way of manifesting Vinnie or Chief Hayes busting through the greenhouse doors to arrest Brian for his crimes.

No one came bursting through as Brian

continued to chop and slash. Hiding behind the roses' defenses would only buy me so much time. His accomplice was on the way, and I needed to be gone before they showed up. But I had no idea where they were coming from or how long it would take them to get here. I needed to go on the offensive.

I reached out my right hand, winding my fingers through the leaves and pressed the pads of my fingers to the closest rose. I blinked and the room tinted red as I saw through the plant's perspective. It was enough to alert me to the fact there were rows of vibrant yellow roses along the wall closest to the door outside of Brian's field of vision.

Sustaining the barrier and coaxing the yellow roses into the fight strained my abilities, but I didn't have a choice. I used my free hand to direct the second set of flowers to form a large wreath, wide enough to wrap around Brian's body and secure his arms to his sides. Through the cuts he'd made in the barrier, I saw the bottom edge of a bandage on his forearm. I hadn't noticed it before. The thorns dug into his skin, tearing the bandage, and reopening whatever wound he'd sustained. Somehow, I managed to reanimate the vine I'd created, and it looped around his ankles, cinching them tight. He yelped as his balance went out from under him. I felt more than saw the blade of the machete lodge into the barrier mere inches from my chest.

I was vaguely aware of footsteps pounding on the ground and the door to the greenhouse slamming open. "Police, don't move!"

Vinnie's voice was sharp and clear. It filled me with so much relief that I sunk to the ground, letting the flowers fall. The barrier wilted before me, and my head grew heavy from the exertion. I slumped sideways into a pair of strong arms and turned to find Chief Hayes behind me.

Where'd he come from?

"He was harvesting human organs," I said as the room began to spin.

"There will be time for all of that later. Let's get you out of here," Chief Hayes said.

"Brian Beekman, you are under arrest for the assault and kidnapping of Darcy Ingram," Vinnie said, beginning to free Brian from his floral bonds and replace them with handcuffs.

And for the second time that afternoon, a man carried me through the door of the green house. This time, though, I didn't feel like I was being carried to my death. I didn't have the energy to ask where the chief was taking me. I just let him take me. I ended up in the back of an ambulance with someone poking and prodding the lump on the back of my head I'd nearly forgotten about. A second medic shoved an oxygen mask over my nose and mouth. The exhaustion from fueling so much magic settled over me like a weighted blanket and I succumbed to the ache in my head, closing my eyes and settling into unconsciousness. The sirens of the ambulance wailed overhead as they took me to the hospital and away from Brian and his greenhouse, but they sounded faint to my ears.

15

I came to in a hospital room, the harsh overhead lighting blinding me as I opened my eyes. Machines beeped around me, and I felt something poking in my nose. I reached down to tug a nasal canula free, setting off an alarm. Shoes squeaked on the linoleum flooring and a scrub-clad nurse appeared in the doorway to my room.

"Oh, you're awake," she said, approaching the side of the bed. "You need to keep this on."

She tried to put the canula back in, but I pushed her off. "Stop. I'm fine. How long was I out?"

"Medics brought you in about an hour ago," she answered, still trying to push my hands away.

"Sylvia, let her be," a familiar voice said from behind the nurse.

I craned my neck to find Vinnie standing there and I relaxed. Syliva cast Vinnie an annoyed look, but stopped trying to force the extra oxygen on me. She turned back to me and pointed to the other monitors. "Leave those in place until the doctor discharges you."

"Sure," I answered and watched her leave the room.

I did my best to sit up straighter as Vinnie took her place at my bedside. "Did Brian tell you anything?"

"He's with Chief Hayes now. Rick will get what he can out of him. But Darcy, what were you thinking? Going there alone!"

"I didn't expect to find human body parts in a freezer," I retorted. "And I called you right away."

"You broke into the man's shop."

"The back door was open," I said. "I just went in the non-public entrance."

"You're lucky he didn't hurt you."

"I'm not as helpless as you think," I said.

"Believe me, I know that now." He gave me an almost admiring look. "I'd heard talk that you could do things with plants, but that was ... that was something else."

"It's not something I share with most people. To

be honest, I've only really known I had these abilities for about a year, and it wasn't until I moved here that I started learning to control them."

"I know I'm supposed to be taking your statement right now, but can I ask, is it just roses?"

I shook my head. "All plants. I can control them and make them grow in different ways. Sometimes, I can even see through them. When my magic first showed up, I could only hear the plants. They were like little voices in my head whispering what they could be."

"You working for Sage makes so much more sense now."

"Please, I need to get out of here. Tania's still missing and Brian was working with someone. He called them. He wanted them to get rid of me."

"We are doing everything we can. But you just went through an ordeal, Darcy. You need to recover."

"I need to be looking for Tania. Please, Vinnie, do whatever you can to get me out of here faster."

"I'll talk to the doctors. But I can still take your statement here."

I shook my head. "No. I'd feel more comfortable doing it at the station."

He gave me a skeptical look. "This isn't just so you can see what Rick is doing is it?"

I pressed my right hand to my chest, feigning indignation. "Vinnie, you offend me."

Vinnie let out a long sigh, but nodded. "Okay, let me see if I can urge them along. But I don't blame them for wanting to monitor you with that lump on your head."

The moment he mentioned it, the back of my head throbbed uncomfortably. "It's not that bad," I lied. I'd do anything to get out of here.

"Just promise to stay here until I get back."

I waved my other hand connected to the monitors. "I'm pretty sure Sylvia would pounce on me if I tried to leave."

That earned a smile as he left me alone in the room. As I laid there amid the steady beeping of the monitors, I reflected on how I'd ended up here. Maybe if I hadn't gotten into an argument with Sam, he would have stayed with me when I'd gone to check out Brian's shop. Or if I'd gone back to get Beau, I could have hidden my entry altogether and he wouldn't have even seen me. Though I couldn't change what happened now.

"I can't believe you got kidnapped," Sam's voice was loud in my ear.

I jumped, the pulse monitor giving an angry beep at the sudden change in rhythm. I gave the ghost a healthy dose of side eye as I settled back against the pillows.

"Well maybe I wouldn't have been if you hadn't flounced off," I retorted.

"Oh sure, blame the incorporeal guy for everything."

I forced myself to take a deep breath, letting it out over a count of five. "I'm sorry. I'm just worried. I got the feeling Chief Hayes hasn't been able to get Brian to give up Tania's location. And the longer she's missing, the more I can't help but fear we won't get her back."

"And maybe I'm feeling a little guilty for leaving you. If I'd been there, maybe you wouldn't be lying in a hospital bed," he replied, the anger ebbing from his tone.

"At the very least, we solved the police's ongoing investigation into the people with missing organs."

"You still think Brian Beekman's a vampire?"

"He works somewhere cold that would conceal the fact his body temperature is low. He stays out of the sun, and I think we can safely say he was the one chopping people up like prime cuts of meat for the highest bidder. And I didn't hear him come up behind me so I'd say he can move pretty bloody fast."

"Did he try to bite you?"

"No." As I replayed the interaction over in my mind, I realized it seemed that Brian was not the one in control of the partnership. He was the one left to clean things up after the fact. Besides, if he really had supernatural speed, he wouldn't have come at me with a machete or wasted time trying to hack through my thorny barrier.

"You didn't happen to go looking for me, did you?" I turned in the bed to face Sam straight on.

He hung his head and wouldn't make eye contact with me. "No. I was mad. It was childish of me."

That meant I had no idea about the identity of Brian's accomplice. And I still didn't have a definitive connection between him and the victims, other than that he'd admitted to disposing of their bodies. So, maybe he wasn't the point of first contact?

"I'm fine. It's in the past. Look, you should probably go home to let Beau know I'm all right. I need to get to the station and give my statement ... then try to find a way to track Tania down."

"You know you shouldn't be doing this alone," he reminded me.

"I won't be. If I find anything useful, I swear I'll get you or Beau or Maggie before I go running off to save the day."

"You better." He disappeared into thin air just as Vinnie stuck his head in through the open doorway.

"Good news. They're going to discharge you."

"Why do I get the sense there's also bad news attached to this?" I replied.

"You have to come with me straight to the station and then I have to make sure you're with someone who can watch you for symptoms of a concussion."

"Lucky for both of us my girlfriend's a healer."

"Sylvia will be by in a few minutes to get you discharged. I'll wait for you in the lobby."

I offered a thumbs up and waited. True to Vinnie's word, Sylvia appeared not five minutes later and unhooked me from the monitors. "You should follow up with your primary care doctor if you still have symptoms after a few days."

"Thanks. I'll do that." I took the packet of discharge paperwork and made my way down to the lobby.

Vinnie waited there, pacing the length of the space and his shoulders visibly relaxed when he saw me approaching. I would be lying if I said it didn't hurt just a little that he thought I'd pull a runner on him.

"Let's go," I said and made my way out of the hospital.

WALKING INTO THE STATION SENT A JOLT OF ENERGY through me. Intellectually I knew Brian was in the interview room, being grilled by Chief Hayes. He couldn't hurt me, and our paths wouldn't cross. Yet I still found myself uneasy and anxious about sharing the same space with the man. I'd gotten the upper hand in our confrontation. If he'd taken me anywhere but a greenhouse, the tables would have been turned against me.

I sat in the seat beside Vinnie's desk and waited for him to get situated. He disappeared into the back of the station—probably to report to Chief Hayes that I was here, ready to give my statement—leaving me alone. I studied the evidence board from where I sat. The only change since I'd taken the picture the other day was a small spot at the far end for Ronnie. There were question marks regarding whether he was actually connected to the larger case. I still couldn't say for certain if he was. But I did note that he shared the same blood type as the other victims.

Perhaps Maggie and I had simply gotten to him before Brian and his accomplice could kill him and harvest his organs. At that moment, a realization hit me. Brian's accomplice could be on Haven Island. If Ronnie truly was connected to the other deaths, then that had to be the case.

I reached for my phone, only to realize I didn't have it. I vaguely recalled my hand going numb and the device hitting the floor in Brian's shop. Was it still there? Had Vinnie gone there to search for me and found it? Had Brian gotten rid of it?

"You okay, Darcy?" Vinnie asked as he reappeared.

"My phone. I don't know what happened to it."

"We didn't find it at the greenhouse or the butcher shop. Sorry."

"Thanks. Guess I'll have to get a new one."

"My guess is he got rid of it somewhere between the shop and the greenhouse."

"I don't even know where that was," I said.

"His parents' property," Vinnie answered.

He'd said his mother had liked flowers and kept them in the shop to ward off the scent of blood. Had he maintained the flowers in memory of her after all these years?

"Are you ready to give your statement?" Vinnie sat, fingers poised over the computer keyboard.

"Suppose we ought to." I couldn't help glancing in the direction of the interview room.

"The minute we get something actionable, we'll jump on it," Vinnie promised.

"I know," I murmured.

I tried to focus on recounting the events that had led me to being in the hospital. I left out my visit to Devina. He didn't need to know I'd been looking into vampires. Then again, he'd been understanding of my magic.

"So, based on your discussions with Maggie and visiting the shop, you believed Brian had been the one to attack her and take Tania?"

"Yeah. And we found that cloth with the butcher shop logo on it when they Maggie's car turned up."

"And instead of contacting the police first, you decided to investigate on your own."

"I know how busy you've been. Vinnie, you've hardly slept in days and neither has the chief. But I did call you when I found something."

"And what led you to discover the freezer?"

"It was making a different sound than the others. I didn't go there expecting to find that. I was honestly hoping I'd find a clue that would point me to Tania's location. That's why I called you when I realized what was there."

"And after he knocked you out, what then?"

"I came to in the back of a freezer truck. I

pretended to be unconscious when he carried me into the greenhouse. But he realized pretty fast I was awake. He called someone to come deal with me. It sounded like he'd been working with someone."

"Working with someone?" Vinnie repeated.

"Like an accomplice. I don't know, it sounded almost like Brian was the weaker one in the relationship. I didn't hear any of the conversation except what Brian said."

"And then you used your magic to subdue him."

"Yes. Though, uh, you might want to leave that part out."

His cheeks flushed a little at the suggestion and he stared at the screen for a moment before letting his fingers fly over the keys. "I'll finesse it," he finally said and printed the statement. "Give me a minute to grab this."

He bypassed Chief Hayes' office—even though I could hear the printer within whirring to life—and darted down the hall. They clearly hadn't realized Brian was working with someone. Maybe now Chief Hayes could apply enough pressure to get Brian to talk.

Behind me, the automatic doors whooshed open. I turned to find Maggie running in, cheeks flushed and a determined glint in her eye. She marched over to me, pulled me out of the seat and wrapped me in a fierce embrace.

"Sam told me what happened. I had no idea. Darcy, you could have died!"

"I know. I'm sorry. I shouldn't have gone off alone. I know I promised you I wouldn't, but I thought I knew what I was doing."

"I've been trying to call you, but you haven't answered," she continued, stepping back to examine me.

"I think Brian tossed my phone on the way to his parents' place. He took me to a greenhouse full of roses."

Maggie gave a soft, nervous laugh. "That was his second mistake."

I quirked my head to the side. "Second? What was his first?"

"Messing with my girlfriend."

"I don't think Chief Hayes is having much luck getting him to talk. But I know Brian's been working with someone. He called them to come deal with me."

"Thank goodness Vinnie and Rick got to you first then." She kissed me before whispering, "I found something else that might help us get Tania back."

On cue, Vinnie returned, stepping into the

chief's office to grab my statement. I practically snatched it from his outstretched hand, read the summary, and scribbled my signature at the bottom. I was getting far too comfortable with giving these statements.

"She's under doctor's orders to be with someone who can monitor her for concussion symptoms," Vinnie addressed Maggie.

"I won't let her out of my sight," Maggie promised, before looping one arm through mine and dragging me out of the station.

"What did you find?" I pressed once we were out of earshot of the station.

"All of the people that turned up dead and missing organs, well I didn't recognize them from the clinic. I'd seen one or two of them for a flu shot, but not recently. But they'd all come through the hospital in the ER when I'd been shadowing Dr. Fitz."

16

I must have heard Maggie wrong. "But he's a doctor. He helped look after Piper when she fell into that magical coma."

"I'm not saying he did anything, but after I checked my records at the clinic, I went back to the hospital and checked the list of patients I saw on rotation during the timeframe the victims showed up dead. They all fit."

"What did they come in for? Was it all the same thing?"

"No. Some of it was things like acid reflux or stomach pain. One person was having blurred vision and vertigo. Nothing that should have been fatal."

"How was Dr. Fitz with the patients? Did he do or say anything suspicious?"

Maggie rubbed at her temples. "Not that I remember. Everything seemed normal. He didn't spend a lot of time with them, but he had access to their charts. Most of them did get bloodwork done. And honestly given that it was overnight I wasn't paying attention to all the tests he had run."

We continued walking toward the B&B. "You think he took extra samples? To do what?"

"I don't know."

"Did you ever notice anything that might suggest he wasn't human?"

She stopped walking. "You think he's a vampire?"

"Maybe? We know that Beau has been sensing something hunting in town for weeks and vampires ae real. I talked to Devina, and it looks like there's one in town. Or at least there was one a few years back when they tried to turn her."

"I can't say I ever noticed that he was off in any way," Maggie finally answered as we reached the front steps of the B&B. "I guess his hands could have been a little cold, but aren't most doctors?"

"Have you ever seen him work the day shift?" I pressed as I led the way inside and through to the kitchen.

"Well, no, but I never did day shifts either. And

they always need people to work overnight. It's not exactly the most desirable shift," Maggie answered.

"But it would be perfect for someone trying to avoid being out in daylight," I said.

"Who are we speculating about now?" Sam materialized beside the sink.

"Darcy thinks Dr. Fitz is a vampire," Maggie answered.

"You said yourself he crossed paths with all of the patients," I reminded her.

"I still don't get why he'd want to kill people for their organs," she noted with a sigh.

I didn't either, but maybe we were looking at two separate crimes? It was possible Dr. Fitz had some other reason to target them. "What if Brian really was the one behind the organ harvesting and Dr. Fitz just gave him the people?"

"That still doesn't explain why he'd do it in the first place. If he's a vampire, couldn't he just wipe their memory after he fed on them?"

"Devina said they don't necessarily have that ability," I said.

"What are the odds there's more than one vampire in town?" Sam interjected.

"Probably pretty low. I mean, you're the only ghost I've met in town," I answered.

"We could sit here speculating all day, but why not just talk to the man and see for ourselves," Maggie said.

A memory nagged me in the back of my mind. Something I'd overheard at the hospital. What was it?

"I think he's been away for a few days," I blurted, earning a skeptical look from both of my companions. "While I was in the lobby waiting for you to be discharged, I overheard a couple of nurses talking about how a doctor was out, because a relative was ill. A father maybe?"

"We didn't really talk about much personal things," Maggie said.

"You had to have, because he knew who I was. He told me you talked about us a lot."

"I mean he didn't share much about his personal life. He was more interested in the medicine and diagnosing the patients."

"Did he and Brian Beekman know each other?" I began to pace from the kitchen door to the sink and back again.

Maggie tilted her head in thought before her eyes went wide. "I don't know if they were friendly, but Dr. Fitz treated Brian the day we went on our weekend getaway. He was stitching up a cut on his arm when you came to get me."

"That explains the bandage I saw on his arm earlier. Did he say how he got it?"

"No, I was finishing up with another patient when they did Brian's intake."

Things were finally falling into place in my head. If it was in fact Dr. Fitz who was the vampire and not Brian, then maybe Brain knew the good doctor's secret and agreed to keep quiet if ... he provided Brian with bodies he could harvest for viable organs to sell? But Brookhaven was an accepting place. Surely a vampire wouldn't have been maligned here.

"You've got a weird look on your face," Sam said unhelpfully.

"I was just thinking. If Brian found out Dr. Fitz is a vampire three years ago, maybe he was blackmailing him to keep his secret. But then I thought that would be silly since Brookhaven is the safest place I've ever seen to learn magic and to be open about being different."

"Not everyone is as accepting of supernaturals," Maggie said.

Sam waggled his translucent fingers at me. "You do remember the whole argument about vampires we had."

"It just feels wrong to treat someone differently just because they aren't a witch."

"I hate to tell you this, but discrimination isn't just reserved for mundanes," Maggie said with a somber expression.

"So, what do we with all of this new-found information?" Sam said, redirecting the conversation.

I looked at Maggie. "Do you think you could figure out if Dr. Fitz has an ill family member, he might be taking care of?"

"If I looked into his records at the hospital, probably. But that's not entirely legal."

"I know."

"I'd need half an hour."

"Good. I need to run a couple of quick errands and I'll be back."

"Uh-uh, I believe I told Vinnie I wasn't letting you out of my sight," Maggie said, snagging my wrist and pulling me close before I could move to the doorway.

"But we need to divide and conquer. There are still a few things I don't quite understand yet."

"What would these errands entail?" Maggie pressed.

"I just need to ask Devina a few questions and see if there's anything else Ginny can tell me about either Beekman or Dr. Fitz that might point us in the right direction."

Maggie passed me her phone. "You can call Devina. We'll see Ginny together."

The determined expression on my girlfriend's face told me I wasn't getting out of it that easily. So, I opened a browser tab on the phone and pulled up Devina's website to find her phone number at the bottom of the page. Maggie, who had retrieved her laptop in the intervening time between when I'd been kidnapped and now, set about getting into the hospital's staff records.

I moved to the dining room; phone pressed to my ear as the line rang. I was about to lose hope of an answer after the fifth ring when someone finally picked up.

"Who is this?"

"Uh, Devina, hi, it's Darcy. We spoke earlier at your house."

"Oh, yes. Sorry, you caught me at a bad time. After your visit I was struck with an absolutely splitting headache."

"I'm sorry to bother you, but I had a couple of questions I was hoping you wouldn't mind answering. It will help us find Tania."

"If I can, I'll answer."

"Do vampires have to drink a certain blood type, if they're drinking human blood I mean."

"No. but they can sense the difference in blood types. I picked up that little skill, too unfortunately. Partly why I don't go out much. It can be absolutely overwhelming."

"That's good to know."

"What do you really want to ask me?"

"I need to know who tried to turn you."

"That's deeply personal."

"It could be the difference between Tania coming home alive or not. I know it's painful for you to think about, but please, I need to know."

"I told you that in order to be turned you need to be close to death. I'd been in an accident. I was badly injured and the doctor on call offered me the chance to make it through. I accepted. My body healed, but that long life eluded me."

"Was it Dr. Elijah Fitz?"

The line went quiet, which was an answer all by itself. "Yes."

"The accident, was anyone else involved?"

"Yes. It was a head-on collision The other driver didn't make it."

A horrible thought filled my mind. "Was it Susan Beekman?"

"Now who is the mind reader."

"Do you know if Brian or his father saw Dr. Fitz give you the chance to live?"

"I don't know. I was out of it for days afterwards. It's possible, but I never asked."

"Did Dr. Fitz ever follow up with you when it didn't work?"

"For a while he tracked my healing progress. But I think he lost interest in me once I didn't prove to be a successful experiment."

"Did he ever threaten you or offer you anything to keep quiet about the truth?"

"I think once he realized I wasn't going out in public he left me alone. If he knows about my business, he hasn't' said anything in years."

"This has all been really helpful. Thank you."

"Oh, there is one thing you should know," she said before I could end the call.

"Yes?"

"You have a way to find Tania. It's been there all along. You just need to let it lead you."

The line went dead, and I stared at the phone as the call ended. What did she mean? She'd sounded so confident that I would understand her message and yet I was clueless.

"Hey Darcy, come in here," Maggie called.

"Unless I'm mistaken, that didn't take half an hour," I commented as I returned to the kitchen.

"Don't praise me too much. The hospital system isn't very secure," Maggie answered.

I peered over her shoulder as she pointed out Dr. Fitz's file. It had a photo of him that looked eerily similar to how he looked now, even though based on the information on the screen, he'd been hired nearly a decade ago. Had he been a vampire that long? And who had turned him?

"Find anything about next of kin?"

"Yes, it looks like his father is still alive. A Rupert Fitz. There's a phone number listed, but no address," Maggie answered.

"Can't you just do a public search for his address?"

"I can try."

She opened a new browser and did an internet search for 'Rupert Fitz Brookhaven MA.' One address came up for someone matching that name on Haven Island. Why did I recognize it?

"Did Devina give you what you were looking for?" Maggie interrupted my train of thought as I tried to puzzle out why the address looked familiar.

"She said that vampires can smell blood types which might explain why everyone taken had the same blood type, but they don't need to drink a specific blood type. And she told me that I have a way to find Tania."

"Which is?"

"I don't know. She said it would lead me to her, but she didn't give me anything more than that."

"Well, did you talk about anything that might make her believe you'd know what she meant?"

"No."

"You've found lost people before," Sam interjected, still hovering by the sink.

'*Tyson.*'

Beau's voice was a welcome sound in my head. He appeared on the counter next to Sam. I was about to ask what he meant when the answer hit so hard it could have knocked me down.

"Of course!"

"Want to fill the rest of us in?" Maggie shut her laptop.

"When we were trying to find Janice's killer back in March, Piper and I went to Tyson and he gave us this sort of homing device, a stone that let us track people. I still have it."

"Well, what are we waiting for?" Maggie made a shooing motion.

I bounded upstairs to my room and dug through

my night table drawer, finally locating the stone in the very back of the drawer. Why hadn't I thought of this sooner?

It didn't matter now. We had a way to get to Tania now. It had been stronger when fueled by my magic in conjunction with Piper's. So, maybe it would work the same with Maggie.

"Okay, let's go," I said, not bothering to enter the kitchen again.

"Do you know where we need to start?" Maggie called as she ran after me.

"The last place we know she was. Your car at the docks, where Bruce Beekman docks his boat."

We took off at a flat out sprint to the docks, both skidding to a halt at the far end of the pier. Though the spot where I'd have expected the boat to be was empty. There wasn't time to try and find someone to charter a boat to haul us all over creation. But I realized we didn't need them to.

"I think we should look on Haven Island. That's where Rupert Fitz lives and where Ronnie was attacked. She has to be there."

"It's a big island, Darcy," Maggie pointed out.

I held up the stone. "And we've got a way to narrow it down. We just need a boat."

"I thought you might go off on your own again,"

Vinnie called from behind us. He looked at Maggie. "I thought you were keeping Darcy out of trouble."

"I said I wouldn't let her out of my sight. And I haven't. We think we know where Tania is."

"Brian Beekman clammed up when Rick mentioned we knew he had a partner. He's either terrified or loyal to this person. So, he's a dead end. If you think you've got something else to get us to her, I'm all for it."

"Hope you aren't going to object a little magic."

"If it wraps up this case and brings Tania home safe, I'll follow smoke signals," Vinnie answered just as a police boat pulled up to the dock. "Come on. Let's go save our friend."

Time to face off with a vampire.

17

I leaned against the side rail of the police boat as it cut through the water, bringing us closer to Haven Island. Maggie stood beside me, one hand wrapped around the rail, the other gripping my shoulder. My head ached dully in time to the hum of the motor, reminding me it had only been a few hours since I'd been duct-taped and held captive.

"Anything?" she glanced down at the stone in my outstretched palm.

We'd only been on the water a few minutes, but the moment we stepped aboard I'd been trying to use the stone to track Tania. It had done nothing.

"I don't think it works over water." I didn't want to admit that I was worried my body was trying to split focus between healing my injuries and fueling the spell.

Maggie leaned over to call back to Vinnie and the driver. "Can this thing go any faster?"

"It's going as fast as it can. And I know you're not cops, but I'm pretty sure you're familiar with the element of surprise," Vinnie replied over the howl of the wind generated by the boat's forward momentum.

I pocketed the stone to keep it safe and extricated myself from Maggie's grasp. I pulled myself along the edge of the boat and up to where Vinnie stood, so I didn't have to shout at him over the waves.

"You told Chief Hayes where we're going right?"

Vinnie didn't immediately answer. Not a good sign. "We both need this to be over and I wanted to prove to him that I can handle more complicated cases on my own."

"But you have a way to get in touch with him," I prompted.

He held up the boat's radio. That didn't fill me with confidence. Even if he could reach Rick in a timely fashion, it would still take the chief twenty minutes at best to reach us. Things could go abso- lutely wrong in that amount of time. Unless Chief

Hayes was hiding some preternatural speed I was unaware of.

"Where do you want me to set down," the boat operator addressed Vinnie.

The deputy gave me a look, hoping I'd have some idea of where we needed to be. I didn't have any idea. Or did I?

"Hang on," I told them and retraced my steps back down to Maggie. I bumped her shoulder to get her attention. "Rupert's address feels familiar to me. I can't explain why. It's the street name that's familiar."

Because my girlfriend is a wonderful person, she brought up Rupert's address on her phone. We studied the address together, bent over the phone screen.

"Oh, oh of course," I groaned as I mouthed the street name under my breath.

"What? What am I not seeing?" Maggie prodded.

"The mansion where we stayed this weekend. It's across the street from this address."

She thought about it for a moment, but her eyes brightened. "You're right."

I knew where we needed to dock the boat now. I hurried back to Vinnie and the boat operator and gestured to the far side of the shoreline as we approached.

"There's a cove that feeds back into the ocean. It's behind the property we stayed at over the weekend."

"Secluded enough to hide our approach," Vinnie said, giving me an approving smile.

"I'll keep it running," the operator said. "But Deputy you should know the radio's range won't cover the whole island."

"With any luck we won't need it," Vinnie said.

He joined me back on deck beside Maggie. I pulled out the stone again, turning it over in my hand.

"How exactly does this thing work?"

"I think of the person I want to find, sort of feed it some of my magic and it acts like a divining rod." I looked at Maggie. "It seems to work better when there's more than one person's magic used. Especially if both people have a connection to the person you're looking for."

"I'd feed it every last drop of my power if it meant finding Tania," Maggie said.

I caught Vinnie mouth the word power under his breath as he came to the realization he was in the presence of more than one witch. He was getting quite the crash course in magic today.

The boat operator cut the outboard motor and we drifted into the cove without a sound. The boat bobbed in the water a foot from the sand, and I pocketed the stone long enough to get out of the boat and wade through the ankle-high tide to reach the beach. I shivered at the dampness, but pushed on. Tania needed us. Once I stood on solid footing, I took out the stone and held it in my palm. I reached for Maggie's hand.

"Let's bring her home."

Accessing my magic was easy. It funneled from my body and into the stone like a plant soaking up moisture from soil after a hard rain. Warmth crawled up my left arm and flowed through my core and down into my outstretched hand as Maggie shared her power with me.

"I think it's working," Vinnie said in a shocked whisper.

The stone hovered an inch above my hand, and it shimmered brightly when I took a step forward. In short order we made our way across the mansion's property and down the drive. No one appeared to be about thankfully. We didn't need to try and explain our presence to the owners of the house while on a rescue mission.

"Has anyone thought about what we're going to

do when we find her?" Maggie asked as we stood just beyond the gate at the bottom of the driveway. I could see the rosebushes across the road on the Fitz property.

"They've got rosebushes and I think it's obvious roses like me. I'm pretty sure I can convince them to help us slow Dr. Fitz down."

"Hang on, Dr. Elijah Fitz?" Vinnie interrupted.

"Did we neglect to mention Maggie remembered that all of your victims had crossed paths with him in hospital not long before they died?" I said in what was meant as a placating tone.

"You did forget to bring that up.."

"And we think he's a vampire. Capable of super-human strength and agility," Maggie added.

"Should I have brought a wooden stake or holy water?" Vinnie snapped.

I hadn't thought to ask Devina how one actually deterred a vampire. I had to hope my control over plants and the fact we had police back-up would be enough to subdue Dr. Fitz.

I turned my focus to the stone in my hand and watched as it hovered before veering to the left. I hurried in that direction, stopping when I was met by a tall fence reaching a good ten feet up.

"See any way through this?" I asked my companions.

Vinnie took off at a brisk jog, returning a few moments later shaking his head. "It looks like it goes pretty far back."

"And it's too tall to try and climb," Maggie noted.

I spotted some palm fronds on the ground beyond the fence and crouched down, reaching out to them with my magic. They perked up and skittered up to the fencing. The fact nothing caught on fire at least clarified that the fence wasn't electric.

"What are you thinking?" Maggie knelt beside me.

"I'm not sure yet. Give me a minute." I passed her the stone so I could use both hands.

In my mind's eye I pictured what I wanted to happen—the fronds to spread out and break the chain links enough for us to fit through. Bolt cutters would have served the same purpose, but there wasn't time to retrace our steps to the boat. I focused on the image of the fronds breaking through the fence, guiding it with my hands to grow outward and up to my full height.

Metal groaned around me and when I opened my eyes, the fencing had a neat hole big enough for us to cross to the other side. The fronds even covered the severed metal edges to protect us from injury. I ushered Maggie and Vinnie ahead of me. As I passed through, I reached out and pressed my hand to the nearest frond.

"Thank you."

The leaf warmed to my touch, as if acknowledging my gratitude. Sweat popped out on my brow as I caught up to Maggie and returned my attention to finding Tania. I couldn't' repress a shiver as we made our way through the tree line, past the decorative rosebushes planted along the winding driveway up to the three-story house. The exertion of pouring magic into the stone and the fronds made the ache in my skull shift from dull to throbbing.

"What now?" Vinnie asked.

I looked from the stone to Maggie and back. It appeared to be leading us directly to the house. That could be a poor choice to simply approach the front door. I wished we had a better idea of the terrain surrounding the house.

"I guess we get as close to the house as we can and see what we can find," I said.

"I'll take that way," Vinnie said and gestured to the far side of the property, leaving Maggie and I to continue our way through the trees.

"I don't like splitting up," Maggie whispered in my ear as we darted from tree trunk to tree trunk.

"Neither do I."

We made it a few more paces before I heard the cock of a shotgun from ahead of us. We stopped mid-step and looked to see the gardener standing there, leveling a shotgun at us. Seeing him head on this time, I could see the resemblance to Brian.

"Mr. Beekman?" I guessed.

"You're trespassing. He doesn't like trespassers."

"Why don't you take us to him, and we can sort this all out?" I said in a far more confident tone than I felt.

He gestured with the barrel of the shotgun toward the front door which stood open. He must have seen us coming. I had to hope Vinnie hadn't been apprehended, too. Bruce ushered us into the well-appointed entryway of the Fitz mansion and straight to a sitting room where Dr. Fitz stood with his back to us. I looked around, hopeful that Tania would be with him, but he was the room's only occupant.

"Caught these two snooping," Bruce said.

"Thank you, Bruce. You can go," Dr. Fitz said in a cool, detached tone.

"But they need to be dealt with," Bruce argued feebly.

"Mother's roses need tending. That's what you're good for after all."

"Elijah, this is insane," Maggie began.

"Where's Tania?" I added, taking a tentative step forward.

Fitz whirled around to face us and for the first time since I'd met the man, I could see the signs he wasn't entirely human. The points of his canine teeth were elongated, and his pupils were dilated. His skin looked deathly pale in the afternoon light.

"Why couldn't you have just stayed out of this?" He looked at Maggie, as if I hadn't spoken. "I told him it needed to be you. But could that idiot do anything right?"

"You wanted me?" Maggie couldn't hide her confusion.

"You said it yourself; you had the same blood type as all the people that died," I reminded her. "You thought you might have been the real target."

"You are cleverer than I gave you credit for."

"You didn't really think I'd stop until I found my friend?" I retorted.

"Where is Tania?" Maggie repeated my question.

"Your friend is fine."

"I don't believe you," I spat.

"She didn't fit my original plan, but she's done more than I could have expected."

"What's that mean?" I asked.

"It's amazing what someone so empathic can do to curb a dying man's pain." He took a step closer. "Did you know when properly motivated she can even take away pesky negative emotions entirely? Just plucks them right out of your head so you don't have to feel them anymore." He mimed pinching his fingers together as he said 'pluck'.

"Let us see her," Maggie said softly. "You say she's fine. Show us. Help us understand what this is all about."

Fitz let out a harsh bark of laughter. "Is this the part where you tell me that if I'd just been honest with you then you would have willingly helped?"

"I don't know. Maybe. But you didn't give me a chance. Instead, you had my friend abducted and me drugged."

I scoured the room for anything I could tap into. There on the mantle above the fireplace was a single rose in a vase. It looked like the ones Ronnie had stolen from the garden only a few short days ago. I flexed my fingers, trying to reach out to it and connect, so I could see where it had been and what it could reveal.

I caught flashes of images. Tania being carried in and up the stairs by Brian. Fitz coming and going, often in hospital scrubs. But always coming from the second floor.

He might be fast, but I had to take the chance. I took off at a run, barreling up the stairs before either he or Maggie could respond and skidded to a halt on the landing. I tried to control my breathing, to listen for anything that might give me a sense of where to go next. The rose had only been able to give me little hints.

Finally, I picked up on a steady, rhythmic beeping that was all too familiar. Hospital monitors. I followed the sound down the hall and pushed open a door to find a man laying in a hospital bed. The machines were chugging along to keep his vitals in check. Tania sat beside the bed looking pale. I was at her side in seconds, brushing hair out of her face. Her skin was clammy to the touch.

"Tania, can you hear me?" I called, shaking her.

She gave a soft groan, but didn't rouse beyond that. More footsteps thundered on the stairs, then Fitz and Maggie filled the doorway. Maggie shoved her way past him to crouch beside Tania. As she tended to Tania, I studied the man in the bed. I could see large swatches of hospital-grade bandaging poking out from beneath a gown.

"He's ill," I said, turning to face Fitz. "And I'm guessing he's B+? Is that why you targeted those people?"

"He's been in multi-organ failure for months. Too sick for the transplant list. But I can save him. I can find him what he needs."

"Because you're a vampire," I replied.

"Might as well put these skills to use," he said. I picked up on the bitterness in his tone.

"Why not turn him, then?" Maggie interjected.

Dr. Fitz's expression darkened. "It didn't work. It seems my one failing as a vampire is I'm incapable of creating others like me."

Devina wasn't the only failed attempt.

"And the Beekmans? How do they factor into all this?" Maggie demanded as she continued trying to rouse Tania.

"Brian blackmailed you, didn't he? He saw what you tried to do for Devina Coombs. An offer you didn't give his mother."

"So, you've figured it all out. What are you going to do now? You're miles from Brookhaven. You can't do anything."

"You'd be wrong about that," Vinnie said from

the hallway. I could see his gun drawn and aimed at Fitz's back.

"Not as reckless as I thought. Still, it won't help," Fitz replied, baring his fangs. In one fluid motion he spun to face Vinnie and lunged.

The violent crack of a gunshot filled the small room and I instinctively hit the floor. I looked up in time to see Fitz with a neat bullet wound in his upper arm. It hardly bled. Vinnie's eyes went wide as he realized the one thing he had to defend us with had only served to enrage the doctor. Fitz let out an unnatural hiss and grabbed Vinnie by the front of his uniform, slamming him hard against the opposite wall.

Panic washed over me, and I locked on to the one living plant in the space—another rose at Rupert's bedside—and poured all of my magic into it. It exploded in a flurry of petals and thorns as it arced through the air and latched on to Dr. Fitz. It coiled around his torso, inching up until it was tight around his throat.

Before I realized what was happening, Maggie was on her feet, and she'd grabbed Fitz's hands. He let out a garbled scream of pain. I looked down to see she'd somehow given the man blisters. When she stepped back her hands glowed almost as bright as a sunbeam.

"I think now would be a great time to call for that back-up," I told Vinnie as my arms began to shake from sustaining the spell.

"Already on the way," Vinnie replied, gun still trained on the restrained doctor.

It felt like it took hours for Chief Hayes and the paramedics to arrive. Only once Chief Hayes had personally secured Dr. Fitz in handcuffs did I let the magic drop. I collapsed to the floor, losing consciousness again.

18

I was getting really tired of waking up in hospital rooms. When I came to, I found Maggie pacing at the foot of the bed. I reached up to find that this time I didn't have any nasal canula to contest with. Well, Sylvia would be happy I wasn't trying to rip out her equipment this time.

"Where's Tania?" I blurted, catching Maggie off guard.

"She's next door sleeping."

"But she's going to be okay?"

"They're not sure, but they think so."

"Did he feed on her? She was so pale, so weak." I was fighting the blankets keeping me in bed.

"It looks like it was mostly exhaustion. It looked as if she hadn't slept in a few days. Or eaten. They've given her a bunch of fluids and they think rest is what's best for her right now."

"What about Fitz?"

"Rick took him into custody. That's all I know. I'm sure they'll be by to get our statements at some point."

"And yell at us for going rogue," I said.

"Well, you're half right about that," Chief Hayes said from the doorway.

I sat up, no longer trying to get out of bed. "I swear I didn't mean to step on your investigations."

"You never do, Darcy. And yet, you always seem to wind up in the middle of them. But this time, I'm not mad at you. I don't like to admit when I'm wrong … or when I need help, but I'm not sure I would have solved this one without you."

"Has Fitz confessed?"

"He was chatty about his arrangement with Brian Beekman. So, we've got a pretty ironclad case against him for the organ trafficking and a few other crimes. Including what he did to you."

"Fitz was trying to keep his father alive by taking organs from people," I said.

"I'm aware. He will not be hurting anyone else in service of his father ever again."

"You know what he is. How are you going to deal with that?" I pressed.

"Turns out there are facilities that can handle people like him. He'll enjoy the amenities of one such facility pending trial."

"Whatever you need to put him away for the rest of his life, I'll do. He hurt the people I care about and he's not going to get away with it."

"I know you will. If we're lucky, he'll forgo a trial for a lighter sentence." Chief Hayes held up a hand to stop me from interrupting. "Lighter doesn't mean it won't still be appropriate for his crimes. He did abduct and facilitate the death of five people."

"Can we give you our statements once Darcy's released from the hospital?" Maggie interrupted.

"Of course. Once Tania's awake, give her my best."

I hated to think how long my friend would have to sleep to recover from this ordeal.

Tania came home to the B&B after three more days in hospital. I'd busied myself with work, needing the distraction. I felt like a terrible friend since I couldn't bring myself to see Tania in hospital.

Watching her lay there, still so pale, was unnerving. I missed the woman who could sense my emotions before I knew what they were. The friend who could be found in the kitchen, whipping up something delicious all because it calmed her.

"Whatever you need, you just let me know. Or Sam and he'll come find me. Maggie will be here, too," I told Tania as Maggie, and I guided her up the front steps.

"I know I'm an old lady, but I don't need both of you holding onto me like I'm about to fall over," Tania said, trying to bat us away.

"After what you went through, you deserve someone to wait on you hand and foot. And we're going to make sure we do just that," Maggie replied.

"Besides, you're always taking care of other people. It's time we returned the favor."

Sam and Beau were waiting in the kitchen, as was a fresh pot of Maggie's chamomile tea and some freshly baked cookies. Even if Tania wasn't up for eating and drinking, I hoped the familiar scents would be comforting to her.

"I suppose I could do with a little pampering," Tania said and sunk slowly into one of the chairs at the kitchen table.

"You are not allowed to get kidnapped ever

again," Sam said in dramatic fashion. "My ghostly heart couldn't take it."

"Gracias for your concern, Sam. I will try not to get kidnapped again. It was not an enjoyable experience for me either."

Part of me wanted to pepper her with questions about what she'd experienced while locked in Fitz's house with his dying father. But I knew she would share the details when she was ready. Except another part of me hoped she'd just blocked it out; that somehow the chloroform Brian had used to abduct her had been enough to stop her from retaining memories.

The way Tania looked at me suggested she sensed my mixed emotions about her ordeal. It only served to bring on a wave of guilt that even after all she'd gone through, she was still forced to feel others' negative emotions.

"I know you want to know what happened, but I am not ready to talk about it."

"We aren't going to push you. Whenever you're ready," Maggie said, fixing both Sam and I with stern looks.

"We're just happy you're home and safe. And they're not going to hurt anyone ever again," I promised.

"If you don't mind, I'd like to get some sleep in my own bed. Maybe take a shower," Tania said and stood.

I made a move to help her, but she waved me away, moving slowly toward the front of the house and the second floor. I looked at Maggie once Tania was out of earshot.

"She is going to get through this, right?"

"It won't happen overnight, but yes. Trauma can take a very long time to heal. But it will. Not in the way we expect or even hope for, but she'll find her new normal. We all will. We just need to be patient and not push her just because we want the old Tania back."

Patience wasn't always my strength, but I vowed to put in a concerted effort if it meant supporting my friend. But I could rest easy knowing we'd gotten two criminals off the streets and made our little town just that much safer. For now at least, Brookhaven could be a sanctuary once more.

A QUICK AUTHOR'S NOTE

WHEN I STARTED PLANNING OUT THIS STORY, I WASN'T sure I was actually going to take the step and say that vampires were real. But, as I developed the story more and ironed out character motivations, I realized I needed to take that plunge. It just makes the stakes higher and more intense. And I have to admit, I didn't entirely grasp the connection between Dr. Fitz and Brian until I was writing the very end of the book. I'm quite pleased with what I came up with and think it worked quite well.

I enjoyed seeing Maggie and Darcy's relationship progress. It is definitely a slow burn romance but I have a firm trajectory for their romance. It also felt like it was time to put Tania in harm's way. We've seen both Darcy and Maggie in the crosshairs and it felt only right that Tania had her turn in the hot seat. While we didn't see the real effects of her abduction in this book, I can promise they aren't going to be forgotten. There is a lot coming up in the next book that is going to showcase what she went through.

If you noticed a somewhat softer touch from Chief Hayes, you weren't imagining things. Darcy has proven herself to be a useful ally over the last few books and I like to think that he's warming up to her. He's accepted that she's part of his town and the people he's sworn to protect. Plus, both he and Vinnie did really need the assist this time around.

As I said, I have some big emotional payoff plans for the next book. We visit Brookhaven at Halloween-time and it's going to be all kinds of spooky and shenanigans ensue. Plus we get a team-up I've been waiting for since I first conceived of the series!

TURN THE PAGE FOR A GLIMPSE AT DARCY'S NEXT CASE in *High Spirits*...

<u>HIGH SPIRITS</u>

Something spooky this way comes...

When Halloween comes to Brookhaven, Darcy is eager to take part in the town's festivities. Ready to truly share her hedge witch magic, she plans to come out at the big All Hallows Eve Extravaganza. But when townspeople begin acting strangely, she finds herself tangled in another mystery.

Before long, Chief Hayes falls victim to unusual behavior too, leaving Darcy to solve the case without police intervention. Her sleuthing unearths a startling truth: someone's unleashed a powerful spell on the small town. With her allies at risk, Darcy races to find answers.

She soon unmasks the culprit. But when they insist the spell has gone awry, they beg Darcy for help setting things right. If they can't undo the magic and reverse the havoc being wreaked through town before midnight, everyone under the spell will be lost for good.

Scan the QR code to buy High Spirits

ABOUT THE AUTHOR

S.E. Biglow is the pen name of *USA Today* bestselling author Sarah Biglow. She lives in Massachusetts with her husband and son. She is a licensed attorney and spends her days combatting employment discrimination as an Investigator with the Massachusetts Commission Against Discrimination.

You can find an up-to-date list of all my books here

www.ingramcontent.com/pod-product-compliance
Lightning Source LLC
Chambersburg PA
CBHW060817190726
48285CB00002B/697